The Love of
A Hog Hunter

LaMuriel Ojo

The Love of A Hog Hunter

Copyright © 2016 by LaMuriel Ojo

All rights reserved. No part of this book may be reproduced or transmitted in any form or by any means without written permission of the author.

ISBN: 978-0-9855978-2-5

Contents

List of Illustrations

Introduction

They called me "Hog Hunter." I hunted hogs with passion all year round. Popular hog hunting started around the first of September. I was thirteen when my dad introduced me to the wild boar in the back lands of Mayday, a "one-horse town" in Echols County, Georgia, that you'd miss if you blinked your eye.

Echols County was home of the carrot of the south. It had a population of 2000 or so people. My dad farmed and hunted hogs, and his dad before him farmed and hunted hogs. It was our tradition.

At thirteen, my heart skipped a beat when my dad introduced me to hog hunting. But if you were ever going to be respected as man in the Taylor family, you took a spit, grabbed your big, straw-brimmed hat and boots, and walked out the back door into the crossover passage of bravery. You can smell the hogs miles away. The stench is almost as bad as a scared skunk caught up in a car with the windows rolled tight. But you learn to love it—and the hunt, too.

We raised dogs, and I learned how to use them for hog chasing as I became older. When out hunting, my dad and I used two kinds called trail and muscle dogs. A pit bull is a "hot-nose" muscle dog, and he can smell a hog if it just went by, but a trail dog can track him if he went by yesterday or two days later.

My father taught me that you send that trail dog out first. You give him a sniff of his target then let 'em free to go get 'em. Diligently pressing every bush of the ground with his nose down, that trail dog will search until he's on the hog's trail or done cornered him. When his excited barks turn into soprano key howls, then you know he's hit the mark! The next part of the hunt is on target for release of the muscle dogs.

We used three of them. Those muscle dogs would hustle off, barking with their long agile bodies at clocked speeds of 15–20 mph, turning left and right until they reached that wild boar. With their dripping lips and razor-sharp, saber-like teeth, they welcomed the sight of him with fierce barking. This happened in the blink of an eye. Once they had hold of the wild, fighting, mad hog, we'd call the trail dogs back and put them up.

The muscle dogs would be on each ear of the hog— groping, swiping viciously, clenching their victim with those canines till they pin each ear down to the ground and the third dog presses his nose to the earth. We'd rush into the bush, about six of us, sometimes having to use hatchets and machetes to break through the woods and create a trail, always dead set on claiming our catch.

Once reaching the spot, we'd position ourselves around the struggling boar, watching those dogs growling with the huge howling piece of wild meat locked in place, yelping but unable to move. We'd handcuff the hog's right legs to the left. Lifting up that dead weight like ten 100-pound sacks of flour at one time over our shoulders. The four of us would place the hog on the back of the four wheeler and drive to our base.

Then, we would circle and poke each part of the hog. Passing judgement on stature and guessing age and tenderness of the meat, we debated sometimes up to an hour on whether the hog was worth keeping or we should release him back into the wild. Some hogs can weigh up to 1200 pounds, but the heaviest hog our crew has caught weighed 600 pounds. down in Lamar County, Georgia.

My being of existence is the hunt—feeling the hairs stand up on my skin in anticipation, sweat rolling along my brow, stepping in the serenity of the bush, pressing for the final entrapment. This capture keeps me coming back because there's nothing like it; it's the hunt that I never tire of.

Women were like the wild hog, or at one time this was my thought—they were the same as the hunt. Once you picked up their scent and trail, all it took was to lock them down and enjoy them for however long the season would allow. Once in a while, you share them; it didn't matter because sometimes they wanted that.

In the end, I realized that the hunt was more than I perceived. It consumed me on the inside and out.

Before I knew the way to freedom I was handcuffed, hollow, and lifeless on the inner part and it happened a long time ago.

Jamie

Contributors to This Book

My great appreciation to an old friend who gave me the idea for this story from his life lesson. Abundance of gratitude to my husband, Napoleon, to Triniece, my daughter, for her honesty, and to my Aunt Diane for her teaching insight. Many thanks to my mom (Parilee) for a go-getter spirit. Be blessed.

I greatly appreciate all emails about this book at mirrorbuzz99@gmail.com.

Chapter 1

My Life Love and Ten Children

We met by chance on a bridge in Muscogee County, Georgia, one Saturday afternoon in 1950. It was an early September day, with clear skies and temperatures in the seventies, when our paths crossed.

The sun began to dim and duck in the sky, marking the end of another day with the rising of the moon. One could see the rays reflecting off the blue-gray water. There was no cloud cover, just a clear, cool, late evening. Dry leaves rustled to the whistling light breeze that sailed across the atmosphere and tickled the skin hairs.

This weather gave the cats and me the yearning to chase skirts. We rode up like many others to hang out and boogie at the spots nearby. We were having one of our serious moments of jive, leading into another heated debate about whether or not a black man named Horace King built the Moore's Bridge over the Chattahoochee River where we were now walking. The subject caused stuttering, cussing, and finger-pointing. As our voices kept rising during, we bumped into a group of beauties and right into the pathway of my future love.

$$\Longrightarrow\Longleftarrow$$

"Excuse me, ma'am, do you know a bit of history about who built this bridge we're standing on?"

Blocked by his towering presence, Serena stopped in her tracks. Lowering her eyes, she slowly let them inch up from his dark, shiny black shoes to his starched, dark-blue dungarees that hugged his muscular thighs.

She admired his flat stomach and chest anchored by nicely rounded shoulders which held bulging biceps she couldn't dream of getting her fingers around. She finished at the top of his curly ebony black hair, cut close with flawless, cream-chocolate skin cradling light, calico-brown bedroom eyes. Responding to those perfect white teeth with the chipped tooth in the front was easy. A smile sailed off her lips to the baritone voice that gave her goosebumps.

"The man's name is Horace King. He was known for bein' a colored bridge builder."

Jamie spun around to the group, giving a spiteful, loud handclap and quick thumbs up to point at his chest. His coaxing laugh urged more yells and spiteful comments.

Suddenly remembering the appealing informant, he twirled in reverse.

"Hold it a second. Don't split." Shifting his weight to look into a set of light-brown eyes, he said, "The name is Jamie Taylor, and this is Brian and Sean. Where ya'll headed?"

"Oh, just hanging out before goin' to the dance hall down the road at the Juke Joint," she replied. "What 'bout ya'll?"

"No lie—my plans 're no mo' since I saw you, beauty. I'm doin' whatever ya'll doin'." Jamie winked in her direction.

Serena smiled, showing flawless, white teeth, and the romance began. He was eighteen, and she was sixteen. He was filled with charm and adventure compared to her tactful but reserved personality.

Oh, how her breathtaking and sensual presence was drawing me. Serena was draped with unblemished caramel skin, distinctive Cherokee, high cheekbones, and marked with an imperfect hump on her small exquisite nose. Her long lashes over light-brown bedroom eyes balanced the picture-perfect princess. I adored those tight, short-cropped curls styled in a puffy afro and frequently desired to run my fingers through them and massage her scalp.

She stood tall at a voluptuous 5'6" and carried a distinct Georgia pear physique with a petite waistline and great big hips that glided musically and supported her muscular calves. Most times, I would clutch her around the waist, swing my darling into my inner girth for a close dance, and inhale her scent of peaches and cream.

We ventured on our first date immediately the next weekend, yearning to return to each other's arms. It was like a storybook romance that started slowly and emerged into a whirlwind of everlasting love.

As our lips touch under the evening sun, the world felt like it stood still in time, savoring the ecstatic moment— and then the lip lock released slowly for a time to let life commence. My hand clutched hers, as we leaned against the big oak tree which knowingly held many of my secrets while overlooking the dusk on the horizon.

Fate encouraged our bond, succumbing us to the exact spot where our lives touched. The well-traveled Negro-built bridge brought another love triangle together, clasping our seemingly inseparable heartbeat of harmony regardless of my stature almost a foot taller than her. I appeared to love her instantly with every fervor of my being as I crooned at every chance with love-struck eyes.

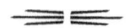

As time went on, Serena could not resist those bed-room eyes outlined with curled lashes looking into her soul and that chipped tooth that seemed to stamp him as sexy and important. The other male interests just faded away to Jamie's irresistible build.

He had such huge, calloused hands that pulled her close to him for big hugs along their slow autumn walks. If the sun could depict their love, it would blaze radiant heat above, causing the wild lilies and daisies to beam and stretch their petal arms outward. Their perfume of sweet nectar would sway in harmony along the fields.

The love triangle continued to evolve as if a bewitching spell were cast. Lately, Jamie seemed inclined to whistle and have a cheerful look on his face everywhere he went. He developed a skip to his step. Poking each other frequently to his attention-grabbing hop, his friends rattled on constantly about how he was "real gone,"

double-struck by a love arrow from the city gal living in Muscogee County.

"Yeah, okay, a fox don' brought me to the knees. I'll say it. Fine. But, these knees will be carryin' fat pockets of bread n' buy anythin' I want to. So flip if you want," Jamie hollered in response to their snickering.

Jamie stayed focused refusing to let anything or anyone scar his relationship with Serena. He worked and prepared for the future. Most nights after working, burning oil into late into the night, studying and making plans to join the US Army Airforce Service. His goal was to be a soldier like his big brother and afterward marry Serena.

Serena's schoolin' was also important, and Jamie was careful not to interrupt. Their dates were very limited and only on the weekends. He kept busy between studies with a part-time job where he picked tobacco and plowed on Mr. Jones' farm three days a week after school. The hours were long from two until sundown, but he had no choice.

Occasionally, Serena would surprise him at work with a basket of sandwiches, cold water, and dessert, which usually included a nice, large piece of sweet potato or egg custard pie. A part of him knew this was her way of assuring he won't forget her and become interested in the gals in the neighborhood that clung to his every move.

Serena needed reassurance that Jamie had lingering magnanimous memories of her since there were big gaps in time between their dates.

What else could explain the colorful bell-looking dresses, with the lacey, tight bustier accenting her small waist and big hips? With every glance, she caused him to drool and place in his mind the wonder of what was beneath. This weekend he would plan something special and hope she was not going to church.

One visit, after popping the final bite of potato custard in his mouth, he was hesitant to move. Serena's head rested on his shoulder, where he would delight in the smell of honey suckle apple scent lotion. Savoring their time together, Jamie shifted his weight closer to hers and pulled her to his chest. Planting a wet, soft kiss on her soft cheek, Jamie boldly asked the question, "Serena, can we step out this weekend?"

She pulled away with widened pupils to gaze at him, lips curled upward and cheeks displaying deep dimples.

"Well . . . let me think?"

It had been almost a month since their last date. The sacrifice for her to come unseen to the city of Mayday from her grandma's country house took 45–60 minutes. However, every time she was with Jamie, he made it worth every bead of perspiration. It was an ache in the bosom now satisfied—for she desperately missed their time together when apart.

"I'm really going to make some studs mad, but okay," she chided.

Jamie's expression showed a big lopsided grin. He liked competition.

"Cool, I'll meet you Friday at the bridge at six p.m. All right? Don't forget now . . . six," Jamie reiterated.

"Okay. Later." Serena hurried away.

Today, her father was in the country at a meeting, so she rode up with him to his mom's and snuck away to see if Jamie was at work. She packed some food just in case. It seemed that all the churches in the area were having private conferences about freedom.

Her father's continuous conversations at the dinner table, explaining that these freedoms led to improved work conditions, better wages, and voting, got tiresome. However, she was glad he was attending them regularly to give her time for these excursions.

It took her forty minutes by foot to get over to where he was working from her friend's house. Bessie would take her on horseback swiftly to her grandma's in enough time not to get snoopy. Her grandmother knew Bessie well since she was knee high. She did not question when Serena would leave or come home with her since Bessie was a devout church girl and smart student. They were also best friends.

It took a great deal of planning to see those famous bedroom eyes of Jamie twinkle at her. Each time he beheld her face, it was as if he peered through her soul with those curly, blue-black lashes. Jamie was worth every bead of sweat and chance.

Serena's feet began to dance along the dirt road onto the wooded, overgrown path. Giggling while spinning in circles, she clutched the now empty picnic basket. Nothing in the world would block her from seeing her love on Friday. The sun appeared to answer her gay mood with gleaming warm rays dancing across her upturned cheeks.

Jamie returned from his break with Serena and continued to work. He assisted on Mr. Jones' farm over the past year to help support his dad and two younger sisters at home. His mother died from tuberculosis in 1940. The pay also left a little jiggle of change in his pocket for his skirt-chasing exploits.

His lips formed a song as he picked up his gloves and walked toward the plow. His spirited whistle sailed a half mile down the straight, consecutive rows of tobacco on the fifty acres of land. Reality reared her head when his foot slipped on the leather straps around the mule's neck and he gave a little jump to regain his posture. He ceased whistling and tightened his lips as he lifted the reigns for the horse to move the plow along the row. He needed this job.

The days seemed to inch by till their set meeting. By Wednesday, Jamie's hands tremored as he was jotting down his grocery list and other needs from the store. In bed Thursday night, he stared at the ceiling, eyes wide open at two a.m., imagining their last soft touch and anticipating her smell and sweet lips.

Squirming deeper down under the covers, he puffed out a couple of deep breaths, fighting to redirect his thoughts. Outside his window, the crickets danced and sung their rock-a-way dance hall music, thankfully disturbing his images with their melodies until he drifted into a welcomed slumber.

Jamie met Serena precisely at six with a huge grin, standing along the bridge that weekend. Many months and seasons had passed since their first encounter.

The lilies returned to cover the field, and lilac buds showered their heads for rebirth. The birds' songs of praise answered the beauty of the afternoon as the smell of sweet nectar filled the air.

She was dressed in a long, flowing pink skirt with thin, white stripes. Her winter-white halter top with square neck was trimmed in long, white lace traveling down to hug her hips. More pale-pink flowers flowed along the edges, and her curly black hair was tucked on the side by a small matching comb.

"You are a sight for sore eyes, beauty," he said, leaning in to swiftly plant one long, wet kiss of sugar on her cheek. "Let's roll?"

Jamie borrowed a friend's work truck for something different, and the silver wheels gleamed against the Ford's black and red color as he proudly led her toward it. They sped along the hair-raising turns and curved dirt roads to his place.

There would be no disturbances because his dad and two sisters were away visiting relatives in Tuskegee, Alabama. They were due for a joyful welcome since one of his sisters was interested in going to visit Tuskegee

Institute and learn more about their renowned nursing program for Negros.

He opened the door and invited her to sit in the back room. Silently, he reached across to the Victoria stand and started the record of "Mona Lisa" by Nat King Cole.

"Can I get you a glass of cherry pop or Muscadine wine?"

"I'll have some pop," she quickly replied. "I love your pad. So neat and warm."

"Thanks. Be right back."

He spun around and dapped with skipping steps to the kitchen, bringing her request back hurriedly.

"It won't be long until dinner, my sweet. Save your appetite."

He rushed into the small cozy with checkered curtains. Jamie's desire was to create the perfect ambiance to let her know he had class.

He took out two white, gold-trimmed plates his mom used in the past for special occasions and placed them on the wooden table covered by a white, lace tablecloth. His friend's wife thought all his effort was "down-right cool" and helped him prepare some of the food.

Placing it on the plates, his mind wondered back to the many Thanksgiving and Christmas holidays when his mother would take him by his hand as a little boy. He would step from chair to chair to place the silverware on the cloth napkins at the table. His mother knew how to be flossy. She was a New Yorker and would frequently tell him all the stories of her days in some of the most beautiful, high-class places with tall ceilings, diamond chandeliers, and velvet seats.

The platters would overflow during those holidays with freshly baked bread, garden-grown vegetables, and hot, barnyard turkey cooked to a perfect brown, just crispy on the edges.

His Mama's famous cornbread dressing hot out the oven made everyone gasp with desire many Thanksgivings. He wiped the tears from the corners of his eyes; the memories felt like yesterday, her last twelve months of misery. He recalled sitting next to her on the bed with cool, moist cloths on her forehead and offering sips of water to her lips as she laid coughing it seemed for hours without catching her breath.

The anger and discord in his chest would accumulate daily holding her and knowing she could not be comforted as she withered away, until finally, her eyes lost their glow and she was gone. He knew she would approve of Serena, his choice wife-to-be. In her, he saw so much of his mother.

"Please join me, madam, in the kitchin." He bowed and held out his arm.

Laughing, she curtsied and grabbed hold of his arm as they entered the kitchen. Jamie pulled out the chair for her to sit. Dancing lights reflected on the dimly lit walls.

"Today, we're havin somethin' good . . . let's see . . . baked chicken and dressin, 'tato salad, fried bread, and for desert, hot apple pie whenever you're ready," he stated in a poor attempt at an Old English accent.

"Mmm—smells good. Need any help wit' anything?"

"No, beauty, just eat up; I don't want you to do nothin' but lay back. I'll handle everything for my special lady."

He disappeared into the kitchen and came back with two glasses of Muscadine wine. Humming a chant of royal welcome, they lifted their wine glasses.

"Here's to a night with my special lady."

Jamie took a big swallow, almost emptying the glass, and abruptly dropped to the floor onto his knees. He positioned his face squarely in the eyes of Serena.

She gasped, drawing back, and almost flipped her chair backward, wine spilling from her tipped glass.

"I'm sorry," he exclaimed.

Jamie pulled her chair toward him and spread a small towel over Serena's lap in one sweep. He looked upward into her widely exposed pupils as she held her lips slightly open, one eyebrow slightly raised. Recognizing she was feeling uncomfortable, Jamie laid his hand on top of hers that was now resting upon her lap.

"It's okay," he said.

He reached to her plate for the fork, filled it with food, and lifted it to the crevice of her lips.

"Let me feed you, my beauty. Please?"

One forkful after another, he brought food to her lips. In between, he told her about his goals in life, and she asked questions about his family and how long they had lived in the house.

"How come you feedin' me? I can do it myself," she said in a soft, wispy voice.

"I know. I'm your servant, Serena; you can git me to do anythin' you like."

He lifted a soft cloth and dabbed the corners of her full lips. Then he sat down opposite her. They continued to joke and laugh.

The smell of apples began to fill the air hours later as they shifted into the backroom where he put on "Mona Lisa" again and drew her hips close in a slow dance. Later, sitting with her on his lap, she insisted on feeding him several bites of apple pie with the last big bite halfway to his opened mouth but ending between her lips.

"So you shootin' me down?"

"Yeah," she said with merriment.

"At least I know you liked the pie. I made it myself," Jamie said.

"It's good, almost better than mine."

Giggling, he stood up.

"Let's have a little more wine."

He snapped his fingers while twirling in a circle, and Serena laughed, "Shake it, sugar!"

Jamie returned all smiles.

"Another toast tonight to you, my beauty . . . I'm thankful we met on that bridge that day. I repeat 'gin, I'm at your service to do whatever you want and get you whatever you need . . . drink up!"

They played card games and emptied the bottle of wine until they both were silly and stumbling. Jamie taught her some of his card-switching street moves. The sweet chords of "Unforgettable" started again on the record player. Their bodies intertwined, his hands grasping her hips and her head upon the crook of his shoulder.

Jamie's lips began to press against her neck, leaving wet imprints that trailed a pattern to the crest of her full lips. She could smell and feel his wine-glazed breath against hers as he sealed their space.

Before she was fully aware, she was out of her clothing and lying on Jamie's bed. The sun had come down, and the moon was dominant in the sky. The crickets were singing their song. By morning time, Serena was a mature woman.

The Meeting

Over time, Serena began to notice some changes in her body. She asked Bessie about it. Coming from a very strict, religious household, many things went unspoken.

"Serena, we need to visit a doctor. Honey, I want to say you knocked up. I just hope you not, Serena!"

"No! I can't be. I timed it, I counted the days, and I'm like clockwork," Serena said.

"We'll go to my cousin's place away from here. She'll know somewhere."

Her cousin took them to a tucked-away clinic nearby where Serena found out she was two months pregnant.

"You have to tell him, Rena—real fast, so ya'll can come up with a plan. Yo' dad is goin' to kill yah."

"I know, I know, don't get flipped . . . okay!"

With tears flowing downward from her swollen brown eyes, Serena gave the news sitting in the front seat of Jamie's Ford.

"Jamie we did something wrong. I'm knocked up. Two months."

Jamie sat in silence, his mind racing with all kinds of thoughts, but he wouldn't dare challenge her in any way. She wasn't easy.

He knew he was her first and only lover. He chose his words carefully, leaning in to wipe teardrops from the lashes of her big brown eyes.

"Serena, everything goin' to be fine. I'll marry you, and we'll be together—forever. I'm not goin' to leave you. You were the one I wanted to marry since the day I turned around and saw you on dat bridge. I love you, Serena, wit' all my heart."

He kissed her lips gently, and she looked at him and smiled. A long breath streamed from her lips as she snuggled close in his arms. Her friends were wrong. He did love her and would take responsibility.

No one else was important or perfect for him but his sweet beauty. She was his first and only love. He was the first to caress her body. No woman could fulfill him and make his heart skip arrhythmical like Serena could.

"We'll come up with a plan. I'll ask your old man for permission for yer hand in marriage."

Jamie knew about responsibility. His father drilled those morals and values in him daily.

"Son, if you a man, act like it—pay yer bills, save yah money, and don't let no one tell yah you ain't good 'nough. Show dem you is."

No one had to beat accountability into him; he would marry her as promised and have a family. They agreed for him to meet her family on Saturday morning. The marriage was to be quick before she started showing in the belly.

As promised, the following Saturday, Jamie came to her house in Muscogee County. The place was a quaint, wooden house with blue shutters and a wrap-around porch with steps in the front. It had five rooms and a lot of land surrounding it. Later, Jamie found out the three acres of land also belonged to Serena's family.

They had chickens with a hen house and a couple of cows and horses. The chimney was going full blast to keep the place warm for the cool mornings. The welcoming aroma of fried bacon met him at the steps.

Serena, sixteen years old, would be the first to finish school and go to college up North. She was completing her final grade studies and would test for college in the spring. She desired to be the first teacher in the family of four children. There were three boys and her.

During the summer, Serena would live with her grandma while going to school for extra studies. Those were the times when Serena would sneak off and regularly be with Jamie. When summer was almost over, she and Jamie made plans to keep their love going strong.

On the return from Mayday to Columbus, her heart ached with despair. Waving goodbye and averting her shoulders straight ahead, she attempted to hold back the pressing tears in the car with her father. They fell upon her cheeks. She would not let Jamie see her love for him as he stood in the distance looking on. Now everything was going nowhere with a baby on the way.

As her dad opened the door, Serena remembered their plan to unfold on the weekend. They rehearsed in detail from beginning to end all night a few days ago. Jamie felt as if he plotted the best strategy.

She was to tell her mom and dad that Jamie was a close friend from summer school, visiting in the area looking at colleges, and she invited him to dinner.

It was Saturday morning. Jamie came to the door with the gift of a wild hog he had killed the day before, cut up and cleaned as arranged. He was smoothly dressed and was as serious as a reverend in a pulpit with his blue slacks and starched white shirt with red pinstriped tie. Sporty, shiny, black shoes finished the look. He didn't care for church fellowshipping that much but decided to wear the set of clothes his father forced on him for the three or four times a year when he would go to church. He was glad they still fit from last year.

"Hello, son," Serena's father said from the back door.

"'Mornin', Mr. Whitmore," Jamie rambled off.

"Bobbie, come take this gift of what Jamie brought to the kitchen and show your mama."

"Son," he said, nodding toward Jamie, "take a walk with me."

Hesitantly, he stepped away as Serena's dad exited out the house.

Stepping fast to catch the rhythm, Jamie was slightly behind Serena's father as he trampled down the trail behind their house. Subconsciously, he was rehearsing the big baby news and the exact words they practiced.

Preparing how to share the marriage, Jamie attempted again to match the rhythm as they walked along. Nothing in his head seemed to make sense on how to break the silence as he trotted along. His heart began to beat faster; he might be only eighteen, but he was going to fight for his family, for his one and only love.

"Son, speed up!"

Mr. Whitmore was across the field.

"Yes, sir." Jamie broke into a trot to catch up and walk alongside Mr. Whitmore.

"Jamie Taylor, I know everything about you. I have done my checkin' 'round. You're a keen guy with yer schoolwork and the ladies. I know you only eighteen, but it's too ol' for my daughter and too young to know anything 'bout how tough this life is. You got one brother and two sisters down in Mayday, Georgia. It's been hard on you and yer father since yer mother's death."

Serena's father stopped in his tracks and spun around to look at Jamie, who stood still in front of him.

"I met yer father at one of those freedom meetings down there in Statenville, and we had a long talk 'bout this relationship between you and my daughter. He wants you to go to college at Tuskegee Institute, where ya'll have family. He said yer grades were good 'nough for help to get in. If yah didn't agree to goin' to school, he knew you were goin' to the service like yer olda brother."

Jamie just stood there with his face tightening, his lips pressed together firmly. How could this old man speak about his family and especially his deceased mother so informally and open as if they were friends? Who in the hell did he think he was?

"Why do you want to play around with my gal? Go get you some fast fox till the school term is over." Mr. Whitmore continued without a breath, "I educated myself because there were no good teachers to help me. For her, it is different. She is goin' to be a schoolteacher and, in a few months, the first one to graduate high school in our family. So, I don't want you 'round after today. Go do somethin' wit' yer life, boy. It's seem like you have yer head on straight. You got a good plan with college or service. But don't think I 'aven't heard 'bout your love for the fat city, Mr. Hog Hunter. I know 'bout your family love for hunting hogs and the easy chicks too! You understand me, boy?"

Jamie's back straightened and lips tightened. His hands formed into a fist, itching to knock this old man to the ground. He knew that wasn't the smart move to make.

Jamie took a deep breath in and released the air through his nostrils. Dropping his shoulders, he loosened his hands.

Stumbling over the first words, he slowly replied, "I . . . I hear you sir, but over the last few months things has changed . . ."

A short silence followed by a deep swallow allowed him to continue swiftly, "I have to get married to your daughter because I love her and the baby she is carrying, which is mine."

A rush of air hit his face.

He woke up with bulging black flesh around his right eye and nose and Serena nursing it with a cold cloth. He was a half mile from the house. He did not see Mr. Whitmore's fist come like a jolt of lightning out of nowhere and cold-clock him to the ground.

There was no meal. Mr. Whitmore walked onto the porch when they finally made it from the field. Jamie was sitting along the edge, still nursing a blackened eye.

Three words were all her father managed in a shallow tone: "Go home now."

Jamie got up because of Serena tugging and began walking toward Mr. Whitmore to straighten him out. He did not care who he was; he was not going to take this black eye like a sucker. Serena began to wail and plead as Mr. Whitmore stood his ground and said, "Careful, son, I don't want to hurt you any more than I 'ready have."

"Please, Jamie, just leave! Please, if you love this baby and me . . . Please!" Serena squawked.

Her shrilling scream and the erratic, circular motions with her hands in the air were pointless as Jamie kept marching toward Mr. Whitmore. Finally, she threw her body in between her father and him. Jamie stopped in his assault trail, pulled back his fist, and looked squarely into her lovely face flooded with the wetness of perspiration and tears. He wiped one off her eyelashes and in a whispery voice and said, "Okay, I'm leavin'."

His lips pressed against her forehead briefly, then he turned, walked swiftly down the porch steps to get in his new, two-door black Chevrolet, and spun off.

As the dust flew in the air driving away, Mr. Whitmore continued standing on the porch with his arms crossed and head held low. Serena stood, shaking and sniveling. She prayed that when he reversed out of the yard that their union of love and marriage did not go with it.

Her father did not show a hair of his head for months after the day he unwillingly appeared for the small wedding. He sat in the back pew of the church with a frozen blank expression, back straight as a plywood, arms folded through the entire ceremony two weeks later. Serena's mom, quiet but loving, maintained her relationship with them. She came to their place with clothing and cooked food, always lending a hand to help before and after Jamison, their son, was born eight months later.

Addition of Nine

Once you start hunting wild hogs, you're hooked. I don't know how you couldn't be. I loved hog hunting like I loved my Serena. It was my obsession.

Some people become addicted to alcohol and cigarettes like a buddy of mine called Shine. Homemade moonshine replaced his blood supply, which explained his nickname. But he was a great hunter and tracker and could find Jesus himself if he was in the woods. We live to hunt boars. That's what we do. It's what we know we're good at if nothing else, because our crew grew up hog chasing.

We could tell anyone about how a hog looks from the tail to the tusks. A mature hog can reach 36 inches and weigh over 400 pounds. The hog's body carries long, stiff, scraggly hairs with a lengthy, strait tail and sloped neck. Wild boars have hair color ranging from dark brown or grey to black. I have seen and smelt them all.

I have wrestled and sprinted away from those four fierce tusks that grow from birth to death, with pointy edges on the top and bottom of their mouth. Their razor-sharp tusks can work as carving tools, easily piercing skin or carving up a Thanksgiving turkey effortlessly. The tusks, or otherwise weapons, normally measure 2–3 inches, and those wild boars ground them tusks regularly against the lower ones to produce spiky, jagged edges. This is how you can tell in your chase whether it is a male or female since in the males the tusks are bent upwards.

Hunting for the wild pig gave me the excitement I needed for my adrenaline. I'd admit my two addictions to every one of the fellas anytime: hog hunting and Serena, my love.

I know Serena and I met very early in life. It was like a storybook romance that started slowly and turned into a whirlwind. I loved her with all my heart. She was patient, strong, and beautiful with multiple talents from sewing to cooking to decorating—you know, the gift of creating something from nothing. Who else could turn old, dull, creaky wooden crates into fancy, etched-mahogany shelves with colorful flowers? Take an ordinary wooden butter churner and turn it into a tall, elegant, intricately etched, colorful vase. Serena's knack for creativity transformed pieces of old cloth and sheets into fancy store-brand curtains just by adding a little lace and ribbon.

We didn't get to make many plans, but we both knew we wanted four children: two boys and two girls. We ended up with ten. Just as quickly as one would come out and she would heal, we would have another. The last two pregnancies brought the twins and the baby girl, Monica. We were finished at two girls and eight boys.

A huge land was a necessity for our big family. I knew this after the first boy. Four acres out in Russell County in the sticks was perfect for our growing family. With the help of the hog hunting buddies and my father, a cozy, yellow wooden house with four rooms and a wraparound porch was built. Two years later and after the birth of our fourth child, more rooms and a small wash area was necessary for our sanity due to overcrowding.

We were blissfully happy, Serena and I. We had chickens with a hen house, cows, a large garden with vegetables, and some apple and fig trees that produced well.

Later on, a friendly neighbor bargained with me on a purchase of an old horse and buggy to help Serena and the children easily get to the garden. I desperately needed the car daily to get to work at the textile mill ten miles down the road.

Serena was always patient with the little ones and me. Beauty was not her only good quality. She emitted blessings with her strong will, wit, and creativity that she shared daily. In the home, she utilized many talents from sewing to cooking to decorating. She could produce something from nothing.

More than once, Serena turned old wooden crates into shelves for the children or shoes and toys and a butter churner into flower holders for our special room. Serena made decorations for the walls out of sticks, acorns, and dried flowers. She became so proficient in doing these things and giving them as gifts that she made a name for herself in the town. People started asking her to create fashionable pieces and fancy knickknacks and paid her good money.

While my love delved more into her craftiness, the hunt continued to call my name. She knew the need to hunt was in my blood. Sometimes, I became so consumed in the bush, it would be the next day before my thoughts and adrenaline would settle. She did not complain.

Other women before Serena would complain of the time I spent on the hunt. I repeated many a time, "But to love me, Jamie, means lettin' me hunt the wild hog. That's what I do. If you can't accept that, then you are free to go."

In the beginning, Serena would join in on the hunt every so often. As the children came, we made it a family outing by camping under the stars. After the kill, I would give Serena a piece of the head and she would prepare a hash, slowly cooking the meat from the head and mixing the meat with onions and peppers. Between some bread, it was the best thang your tongue could ask for.

Everyone would have plenty to eat. Oftentimes, they would listen to the storytelling myths of wild pigs and ghosts under the stars. Sometimes, friends of mine would bring their families, too, and good ol' pig jig would take place with dancing, guitar pickin', and roasting sausages to go with the wild tales by the fire.

Serena was comfortable with the hunts as long as Jamie was home for church Sunday mornings. She believed in zealous faith with works, for she was a serious Christian. Daily, the family performed morning prayers before school.

It was Serena's light of goodness and faithful belief in her God day after day, through one storm and another that gave me a desire to develop a relationship, too. His beauty reflected on her daily. There were always songs of praise coming out of her sweet lips. When things turned wrong or became complicated with finances, family, or the children, her famous phrase was "the joy of the Lord is my strength."

We heard hymns daily. All of us knew them, from the youngest child on up. Many days, she would cook and hum "Blessed Assurance," "How Great Thou Art," "Precious Lord," and the notes would linger in the air, encouraging our faith and lifting everyone spirits. Many of my mornings began standing hidden away in the shadows, leaning against the wall, listening to her soprano notes with my eyes closed, and thanking the Lord for her presence in my life.

Over time, I was leading the prayer before eating meals and at bedtime effortlessly before I knew it. I learned how to give my thanks and eventually saw the work of God in our family.

I truly had so much to give God thanks for. How beautiful we looked with each one of us holding hands, going around in a circle from the biggest to the tiny-fisted fingers of the baby being held. It was a sight I'll treasure forever.

My wife was not perfect. Her nerves did get rattled at times. One fact was certain: She would not let me come inside the house with my wild hog hunting clothes. They were stripped and pitched, waiting for her before coming to the porch. As soon as that old, beat-up red truck pulled up near the trees in the back of the outhouse, she would meet me with a change of clothes and a soft kiss on the cheek. Her coy saying was "my hog hunter wins again!"

"You right," I would exclaim.

We would both giggle every time. It never got old. From there she would take the clothes out to the back of the house for special scrubbing. I bathed and got ready in the outhouse before supper most Saturday nights.

Gentle, caring, thoughtful, and special—these were the words I would outwardly proclaim when gazing under the stars in the bush with buddies of mine. Our women were always in the chatter along with our beer after a good hunt.

Those cats of mine usually tell me to shut up because I'm known for killin' they mood of slurring and spewing complaints of women troubles under beer breath and curses.

One early weekend morning, I awoke to the moon still in the sky. I felt wetness on my legs and left side, and threw back the covers to find blood on the sheets and Serena's thighs. Her eyes were closed, but she opened them briefly and murmured jumbled words in a faint sound that I couldn't understand.

I moved swiftly and carried her wrapped in a blanket to the truck. My foot pressing the gas heavily in a daze at suicidal speed, we reached the tiny hospital within thirty minutes.

She did not appear to be in any severe pain, but just sat there leaned over to one side with her head on my lap. The soft, dark blanket covered all the bloody stains of her nightdress.

Within seconds of our entry and the sight of blood now seeping through the blanket, they took her back behind closed doors. She was not conscious at all. Minutes seem like hours. Finally, a white coat and nurse came out, and, as I rose, the two asked me to sit back down. They took a seat in front of me.

"I'm sorry, sir," the doctor stated, "We did all we could do, but she lost so much blood. She passed away from complications of her uterus. She never suffered."

My head began to spin, and the doctor's voice sounded far away. I never knew that I would not hear my Serena's voice again or see those beautiful irises filled with life before she disappeared from this earth.

I just could not accept it. Shaking my head, I passionately exclaimed, "No, you wrong. No, not my Serena . . . you wrong."

The doctor came to his feet.

"I'm sorry, sir. I am very sorry."

I jumped to my feet.

"Say it ain't so. Please, doc, say it ain't so!"

My tall frame then gave away, and I fell to my knees. With a bowed head, I wrapped my arms around my chest, rocking back and forth. Repeatedly, my voice raised with Serena's name to the top of my lungs. I could not see past the wetness. I did not want to.

Soft arms began to cradle my body as I sung out, "Serena, Serena. Serena, my love . . ."

The nurse held me as she motioned for help.

Those words were all I could say for three days in bed, numb, devastated, and sometimes partially comatose looking out the window clutching her pillow.

After that particular hospital demonstration, the doctor prescribed a sedative for me to help with grief. Now back at home, I refused to take it as Dad entered the room with the pills in his hands.

His scraggly voice softly pleaded, "Please take the medicine, son. It'll help you sleep."

I turned my head, with deep, swollen, raccoon-like circles surrounding red-streaked irises, and murmured, "No, Dad. I just don't want nothin'. Just let me 'lone pop, let me 'lone."

He exhaled, squeezed my hand, and I squeezed my eyes shut to the hobble and pound of knocks from the cane as he left. My dad knew grief from his momma's death.

I wanted to feel this pain—the loss—the deep-pitted emptiness. I needed to remember Serena always and that day that I died with her . . . on the inside. We died together.

Chapter 2

The Sitter

The Miles family lived about half a mile down the road. They were a big help to me after Serena passed. A niece from up North was staying with them and needed work. She volunteered to come and babysit for a small fee. Alicia was her name. As time passed, she became an angel for the family. Her babysitting services were needed almost daily.

The set of twins, now six, and youngest girl, only five years old, were vibrant and active. Their love for the outdoors, squirrel-catching, and nature hunts, as well as daily lessons in arithmetic and writing, kept the family busy. Those little ones were always either breaking something or itching to build something. They were a handful for all us, with the oldest boys and their sister helping as much as possible.

Alicia seemed to handle them and their needs well. Everything seemed to be easy for her. She was also easy on the eyes and smelled nice when she came around.

Alicia was thin with caramel skin and a short, brown-haired bob, which cradled her big eyes. There was a small gap in her teeth, giving those full, tanned lips pure sex appeal. She was 5'7" with long, smooth, muscular legs and a body wrapped tight since she loved to run track.

She was twenty-three years old to my thirty years of maturity, but with her flirting, she didn't pay it no mind. I liked her personality along with everything else. The children thought she was fantastic with her bundle of energy and love for sports. The twins and youngest daughter craved her visits.

＝＝

Alicia loved the children, but she secretly desired the daddy more—that's what the rumors were sayin' at least.

His friends all joked, "Alright, hog hunter, causin' some young'un head to swoon with yo' muscles and charm. Hope you can handle it."

"I ain't messin' with her," he said initially. "She is just the babysitter."

"Yeah, sure," one friend would holler.

"And I'm the cook," another would say.

Alicia could not resist his muscular 6'1" frame with broad shoulders and brown skin. She loved his natural sprinkle of gray in the front of his low-cut hair. His chipped tooth seemed to add to the appeal of his pearly whites. Thanks to his hog hunting and constant over timework at the factory, he kept a six-pack and big calves, which kept the women swooning when he passed by.

Alicia was looking forward to calling that package hers. She did not care if he came with ten smaller responsibilities. Two of the boys were graduating in two to three years. The three oldest were also a big help when they were around.

Her goal was to say "I do" and make all the women chasing him jealous. Then maybe the pies and casseroles carried by consoling ladies with their low-cut dresses, fitted shirts, and skin-tight bell bottoms would cease.

It had been one year since the death of Serena. Stretched out on the porch, looking at the stars and moon, the loneliness was creeping in. Desperation for giving the younger ones a stable home was also pressing on his heart. The school did not help with the long list of calls from the teachers complaining about the three youngest ones.

Alicia would have to stay around permanently. The only solution was to ask her on a couple of dates and tie her in with charm and good lovin'. He needed her desperately. He would start this weekend.

"Alicia, I made plans for us to get together if you want today around 8 p.m. The oldest, Jamison, will be back early tonight to watch the kids."

"Okay, that's cool. Should I get flossied up?"

"Yeah, we'll do the town."

By the end of the year, he and Alicia were married. He needed her energy and bubbly attitude permanently for the kids. He just could not raise them alone.

Rebounding

Jamie woke up from another restless night, sweat pouring from the back of his head down to his back and legs. He had reached for her again, his "Serena," and grabbed the pillow she slept on before her death. Jamie held her all night. He was sure he called her name several times, and she heard his voice.

The dream was so remarkably real. My God, he would give up anything to hear her voice say, "Jamie, my hog hunter wins again." He wept and squirmed with desire for her all night. After three years, he still desired his first wife as if they were newlyweds on their wedding night.

He sat up on the side of the bed and quickly covered up his lower half with the covers as Monica, his youngest, ran into the room with her bare belly and short stubby legs, her arms held outward toward her dad, showing eyes bubbling with merriment. He reached down and grabbed her from the floor, lifting her high above his 6'1" frame as he stood up.

"Alicia," he called. Alicia came running with her apron on. She was in the middle of cooking breakfast. The children grew up fast; four were in high school, three in middle school, and the twins and youngest girl in elementary.

"What you need, Jamie? I'm trying to get them fed before the bus come. You're not ready for work yet?"

"I'll be to the table in ten minutes, but here." Jamie pushed Monica, his youngest, to Alicia after a big kiss on the forehead. "Get one of the girls to get her dressed; I'm running late."

Alicia grabbed and lifted Monica up in her arms, still laughing with only her underwear on, and Alicia asked Monica what happened to her nightgown.

As they left the room, Monica hollered, "Love you, Daddy."

He hollered back, "Love you too, my sweet Mona," as he speedily stepped toward the bathroom to wash up for work.

In exactly ten minutes, he was at the kitchen table having coffee, grits, and toast.

"Alicia, can you change the sheets on my bed?"

She looked up and said, "Sure. Another dream, huh?"

Silence and a stiff lip was Jamie's response as he lifted the coffee mug to his lips. With one more swig, she heard the screen door slam shut.

Jamie refused to discuss anything related to his late wife with Alicia. It was unnecessary, and definitely not her business. They hadn't made love in almost a year and never shared a room as husband and wife.

Alicia slept in the far room of the six-bedroom house near Monica the youngest girl and the twin boys, Ray and Jay, so she could hear them when they cried for their mother or experienced nightmares. Jamie made it clear that he did not desire intimacy of a woman sleeping next to him anymore. It was as if he were locked in the past.

Shortly after hearing the truck pull away, Alicia plopped into the nearest seat, her forehead pressed into her palms on the tabletop. After two years of marriage, she felt ten years older.

Jamie was limited in affection from the beginning, but no one would have thought that time would not fix that. How could he not develop affection for her after all this time? More than two years of diapers changes, wiping snotty noses for him, and he did not appreciate any of it.

After the first year, lovemaking was suddenly reduced from three to four nights a week to once or twice. Now, all affection had ceased.

What was so special about this dead woman that keep him in sweat almost every night? Rising from the chair, Alicia walked into the tidy but dark room of Jamie.

"It's time to find some secrets to this mysterious woman," Serena whispered.

Alicia opened the closet he banned everyone from in his room and found Serena's robe still hanging along with boxes of pictures and some of her popular decorative creations.

The gossip she heard in the community was that Serena was very talented and beautiful, so kind and considerate to everyone. It was like the woman was a saint!

Alicia saw the chair in the corner that Jamie would not allow anyone to sit in when she initially started babysitting the children. Thrown across the back, Serena's gown rested over it; she knew because she was aware it was not hers.

Wailing in anguish, Alicia stormed out the room, slamming the door. Who can fight a dead woman's memory?

Alicia was aware of how quickly Serena's death was. It was devastation for the entire family from the rumors that her mother died six months later from a broken heart.

Now it had been three years, and it was time to love the woman who was here, alive—the female raising the dead woman's children! Alicia swung open the screen door to check on the twins and Monica sitting outside on the porch waiting for the school bus.

Jamie should love her as much as he loved his late wife, Serena, and be faithful and caring, like she heard from so many people in town. He was already the best looking man in her entire history and could top sliced bread and apple butter in the bed.

Jamie's caress on a woman could make her toes curl and melt like butter in his arms. No words would be said while within his arms. The strength of his hands like a vice grip and legs long and agile. When their passion had reached the peak, he would hold her for a couple of minutes followed by a kiss on the cheek or lips. Around the time her breath returned, he was up and dressed, grasping the door knob after saying goodnight. He did that in the beginning . . . now, nothing.

The children were off to school, and the school bus pulled away down the dirt road. Serena waved as it rolled away.

The door clicked behind her as she stepped back into the kitchen walking to the tiny TV room. She could breathe for a minute. Collapsing onto the cushion, she stretched her legs over the couch. Her mind went to how she could get out of this dead marriage she had been in for three years. She was tired, and the only consolation she had now was a bottle of Jack she daily visited.

Hopping to her feet, she marched directly to her drawer for the stash of hidden whiskey. Alicia returned quickly to the kitchen for the nearest glass and exhaled as the liquid was released over cubes of ice. She lit up a cigarette, another habit Jamie was unaware of, and began doing the dishes.

A twenty-ounce bottle would last her a week. This is what he turned her to. It was not a good feeling to find forgetfulness in liquor, but it gave her mind a break. The guilt was heavy in her mind on several occasions after being in a drunken stupor alone with the younger children on the weekend. She promised her reflection many times she would not repeat it. But now, she didn't care anymore.

"I'm tired!" she screamed into the silence, her voice echoing throughout the empty rooms, and glass now just empty ice sailed across the room making a mark on impact against the wall, pieces flying all over the wood floor as if to remind her that her life and emotions were a scattered mess. She collapsed over the sink and slid to the floor in tears.

"I'm just so tired, Lord, so tired of lovin' this dead man," she muttered in a slow slurred tone.

Her body yearned for Jamie many nights. Time would erase his fingerprints off her skin and take away the desire for his touch.

He resisted her advances most times until she stopped trying and turned to the bottle and couple of male friends in the neighborhood. Most thought of her and at times called her foolish for marrying a man with so much baggage when she was such a young beautiful woman with no responsibility.

"Alicia!" Jamie yanked the door open almost pulling it off the hinges. "Alicia, where the hell are you?" He walked swiftly, slamming the wall with his fist, zooming through the kitchen into her bedroom without glancing left or right. Continuing to yell out menacing words, he said, "I have received yet another call at work by the social worker from the elementary school, Alicia. I'm tired of your shit!"

It was for Monica, his youngest. Her "Cake and Mommy" occasion was ruined and this was the end of it. Jamie circled back through the kitchen and found her asleep on the floor of the kitchen where she slid and awoke her roughly with his hands, shaking her left and right.

"Alicia . . . Alicia, wake up. I mean now! Look at me!"

She grunted, raising her chin, slowly revealing her red-streaked eyes. Her sour, musky breath met him, as she snarled, "I'm listening, hog man. What you want?"

"Alicia, how could you?" he screeched, hitting the wall behind her. "How could you go to Monica's school drunk and expect me not find out? It is over between us! It has been for a long time, and I want you out of this house today!"

"No, Jamie . . . Please!

"They threatening to take the kids, woman! You gotta go—and today. I'll help you gather all your things and take you anywhere you want to go. But you goin'! No one is going to cause me to lose my kids—especially not you, with your dranking!"

"You did this to me, Jamie. You did, with your condescending, nonchalant cold-heartedness. All you care about is you and your damn kids. Well . . . what about me . . . what about my feelings and all my sacrifices? I have a life and it should matter to you. I want a baby, a husband that loves me and want to make love to me and wake up with me in his arms. Your wife is dead and never coming back, Jamie. She's dead, and I am alive, right here in your presence, working my hands to the bone every day caring about your dead wife's kids, and you couldn't care less if I fell to the floor and died. Go to hell, Jamie! Go to the pits of hell and stay there!"

Jamie raised his hand to slap her, but stopped in mid-air. Taking a deep breath in through his flaring nostrils, he walked toward the door, hissing in a baritone, "Pack your things, woman," and stormed directly out the house.

He snatched the door of his truck open and hopped inside. The thick dust rising left a trail down the drive as his engine and spinning tires spoke of his anger.

She was right; he had ruined her life it seemed, and it was good they were leaving each other. He never considered Alicia his wife, so he was not affectionate or tender to her, let alone faithful. However, he did make sure she did not know about the others. She filled the spot as a motherly figure for his children, especially the young ones, when he could not.

At first, she satisfied his needs, but he cut it off when she started desiring more outward affection like daily hugs and kisses, phone calls during the day to talk about nothing, him holding her after their romps in bed. He was no comforter; he needed it for himself and found it with the women he began to sleep with.

A new one was demanding his attention. Raging Regina—she was the one that required careful handling and watchful eyes. She was different. Bold, bodacious, and luscious, she chased after Jamie with her words and body, and resisting her was taking all the effort he had until today. Maybe it was about time to stop running from her. Especially after the mess that happened just now.

Chapter 3

Raging Regina

Regina was new to the mill. She had been placed on the presser for the past six months. She studied Jamie. The less attention her husband gave, the more her desire for Jamie formulated. It was about time those desires to manifest and be satisfied. The rumors that Jamie was a widower twice reached her ears with pleasure. She knew he was not looking for a serious relationship. Regina began to watch Jamie's every move and learn his daily work pattern.

Initially, he pretended to be unaware of her. However, Regina was like a hawk eyeing her prey. She matched her every move according to his. At each turn, he received an eyeful of her seduction with the winks and play kisses. At times, Regina brushed against his chest with her body.

Previously, he concluded she was beyond bizarre and this contact was irritating. The daily static at home encouraged him to pursue their purposeful meetings with delight. Regina's creativity caused him enthralled him in anticipating what he would see or what she would say on an everyday basis. However, Jamie always played it cool and presented as if uninterested. For now, it was best. This cat-and-mouse game went on for months.

Raging Regina caught his attention at every angle, eyeing him, brushing up against his body while giving an innocent, one-sided grin. He liked the switch of the hunt. The game revived his inward spirit for pursuit.

Initially, he ignored her boldness, but the more he resisted, the more she persisted. Her behavior reminded him of the rush for the wild hog, except Regina was the huntress and Jamie enjoyed being the prey. Her tactics of trickery enthralled him. The more she hungered after him, the more his desire would compile. Now he was at the point of explosion with just a flick of the finger.

"Good morning, Jamie," one of the girls said.

He nodded and replied, "Morning."

The locker slammed shut with a flick of the wrist as he grabbed his required uniform jacket and slipped an arm through.

"Who you covering this morning?" Guy asked.

"Jean, on the presser. She going to be late," Jamie shouted to Guy as he was walking out the locker room in uniform into the noisy breezeway.

"Man, I wish I had yo' skills; you work every machine in here. The big people up top will never let you go."

"I hope not. See yah at break." Jamie threw up his hand.

He had a reputation of being a hard and punctual worker. The bosses loved him and paid him well because he could efficiently work all the machines in the factory. Jamie was faithful due to the pay and flexibility. The bosses were also patient and considerate with him when he needed time off for his family.

Regina walked up and grabbed his neck for a hug as he swung the corner.

"Hi, Jamie. I missed you last night as I was twisting and turning all night," she said.

Jamie replied while removing her claws from his neck, "You should have grabbed the reverend, your husband, and took care of some business."

"He was praying downstairs, so he couldn't handle it," she said.

"Well, you should have joined in and cut it short; it doesn't take much to get your hubby attention if you know how to use your seductive techniques. *Amen* would have quickly come, and *halleluiah* could have taken over."

She giggled and said, "I really want you to find out and get your evaluation on how my moves are." Regina grabbed him and pushed him inside the snack room. Before he could blink, she planted a long, wet kiss on his lips and wrapped her arms around his waist. "I am tired of waiting for you to surrender. Today is the day I get what I want from you, Jamie."

Jamie shoved her hands together and jerked them with both hands. "You belong to someone else, and you can't handle this."

She smiled, and those magnetic dimples came alive on both cheeks. His knees went weak, but he would not let her know it.

"I want you, and I am going to have you," she whispered in his ear.

"Regina, I am not going to interfere with your love for your husband, and you know this."

"Jamie, I can handle this! I am a mature lady. I just want some companionship. My husband doesn't spend time with me. He wakes up with the Bible and goes to sleep with it. Rev is always at the church, and even our two children rarely see him. He doesn't give me what I need." Her bottom lip poked outward while looking at the floor. Her hands were fiddling with the buttons on her plain gray uniform shirt.

Jamie walked away. It took everything within him to do it, but he turned his back and opened the door.

"Jamie, you just going to walk away like that!"

He kept walking. If he didn't, he would end up in a mess. His body was definitely aroused, in fact, overheated, but his mind knew he was doing the right thing. Regina did not bother him for three weeks and even made an effort to avoid him. Jamie thought her obsession with him was over.

Jamie decided to work on his marriage. He would show Alicia the affection she desired. Time brought more clarity into his thinking after he got away when they had their big fight three days ago.

One mile away from the house that day, Jamie pulled off the road onto the grassy shoulder and sat for almost two hours in the bush weeping and thinking why his life was so messed up.

"Serena, why did you leave me, God, why?!"

Wiping his eyes, he blew a breath, then his nose into a handkerchief.

"I've got to save this marriage for the children. I just don't have a choice." Starting up the truck again, he headed back to work.

He knew that if he must save this marriage, maybe not for his sake but for the young'uns, he had to be more affectionate. This was what Alicia desired and was the only way to patch their marriage.

Jamie began preparing a plan on how to release that affection Alicia desperately needed later on that night while relaxing at his hunting friend Shawn's place. He needed one more night to get his head straight.

"Man, you stay in a mess with women," Shawn said.

"Ah, man, shut up and keep the beer coming," Jamie said in a distant voice.

"What you going to do?"

"I don't know, give in maybe, but, man, she got to get some help with that drinkin'."

"Yeah, you right," Shawn admitted, "for dem kids, she got to, or you have no choice but to let her go."

"I know I can't lose my kids. They all I have of Serena. Mona is just like her."

Shawn shook his head in agreement. "Just like. Thank God!"

"Aw, shut up." Jamie threw an empty can at him. "Give me another."

"For a man who don't usually drink, you putting them down." Shawn laughed, tossing him another.

Jamie grinned. "Yep, and better than you, where's my man Shine."

"He is on de way," Shawn said.

By mid-week, Jamie was sure of his decision. The other women had to go. They were affecting his mind and tearing up his household. It wasn't right, and no blessing was coming from it.

A few days later Jamie was sitting at the cherry hardwood table at Alicia's uncle's house. Crying out, he released his emotions as he explained about all of his thoughts and desires to save their relationship to Alicia.

"I am going to be around more often, I promise," Jamie quietly whispered holding her hand. "I really want our relationship to work. You were right; I have been blocking you out. But I'll change if you will. We'll change together."

"I don't know, Jamie, we have so many problems, and you have really hurt me. There is a lot of pain between us."

"I know, 'licia, but we can take it slow, and I promise you will see a change." Jamie let out a sigh of desperation as he took her hand in his to get her to look into his eyes.

"Please . . . let's try again."

"Okay, I am willing to try, Jamie, but only if there is no more women chasin'. I can't take that anymore."

"Of course, there will be no more of dat; I will respect you and our marriage."

"Alright Jamie, and I am willing to start a AA program at the local hospital to help me with the drinking."

"It's done. I will not chase no mo' skirts but yours, my cupcake," he said as he pulled her up from the chair and patted her bottom.

They laughed and kissed.

"Let's go home," he murmured in her ear.

From that day forward, Jamie started visiting Alicia's room at night and waking up there once or twice a week. She allowed these baby steps toward healing for both of them. Things got better for the whole family. Together they attended school functions, and there was laughter and peace between them.

Within six months, Alicia gave Jamie the news that she was pregnant. Jamie cringed in the beginning but never let on that he could not take on another responsibility. The children were ecstatic and many occasions he caught Monica rubbing Alicia's stomach.

The season changed from summer to fall.

Jamie got out of the small, red Chevy truck as Alicia stood on the porch with her belly protruding outright.

"Hey there. How are my two favorite persons?"

Giggling, Alicia said, "Hungry."

"That makes three of us."

"How 'bout some fatback and eggs with biscuits and fig preserves. I'll make it," Jamie exclaimed.

"Perfect," Alicia agreed, lowering her bottom into a chair while hugging her belly.

Jamie washed his hands and began cracking the eggs into a bowl when he heard a piercing cry from behind. He swung around and saw fluid flowing from Alicia's legs down to beneath her chair.

Jamie dropped the egg into the bowl. "It's okay. Let's go. Everything will be fine. Come on."

Giving her a small push into the truck, he slammed the door and hit the gas, prompting the truck to rev loud like thunder. This seemed like déjà vu. He encouraged Alicia with words and pats on the arm to keep the old memories of Serena at bay.

Jamie attempted to inhale the tears of disbelief, but they broke through the dam of his ducts, flowing over while he clutched the back of his head. The news of a stillborn baby was too much. Alicia was already in her fifth month of pregnancy. He could barely handle the pain in his heart. Regardless—he wiped his face and prepared to be the rock of comfort needed for Alicia.

One chilly morning, instead of Alicia waking him with hot coffee, it was Monica, now eleven years old, shaking and beating him to consciousness on his shoulder.

"What . . . what is it? What is going on?" he asked.

"Alicia is sick, Daddy! She ain't opened her door, and you know she doesn't allow us to open it when it's closed. I called her name, but she didn't answer."

"Okay, I'm coming."

He began to get concerned, because it was very unusual that Alicia did not wake up and get the kids ready on a school day. Lately, attending extra sessions of therapy appeared to have improved her acceptance of the loss of the baby almost three months ago.

Jamie slept in his room last night because of a cough and stuffy nose. His heart beat rapidly as he neared her room where there were no lights on. The sun was still down and the breaking of day had not reached the surface of the sky.

He heard one of the older boys shriek as he was walking down the hall and rushed through the slightly opened door to see what was going on. Alicia lifeless body was stretched out across the bright, colorful flowers of her bedspread. She was grayish in color. It took everything in him to turn to his children showing a blank expression as they hovered outside the door where he ordered them when he heard the panic in his son's voice.

"Jamison, take your sister and brothers out of here, and everybody get ready for school. Everything is going to be okay."

"But, Dad, is she okay, is she living?"

"I'm going to take care of her, don't worry—you know 'licia don't play about your schoolin'. Now go get ready!" Jamie sternly spoke.

Jamison hurriedly shuffled his brothers and sisters down the hall to get ready and out the house in time for the bus to school. Jamie went to the telephone and dialed 911 when he heard the bus pull away.

Alicia died in her sleep. It was exactly three months after the loss of their baby. He did not quite understand, but Jamie suspected that alcoholism was a contributor to her heart failing. She could not take the sorrow of the unborn child. He'd seen the bottles in the trash but did not mentioned it, hoping time would heal the wounds along with the AA meetings.

He went back into her bedroom, sat down next to her body, and bowed his head. Wetness slowly descended his cheek, across the hump of his nose, and fell into his hand. Death was visiting too much in this house—*my God, why?*

After Alicia, Jamie was determined never to let his heart love again. He had loss Serena, now Alicia, and even though he did not love Alicia in the same way as his first wife, he had cared for her deeply. Now she was gone.

"I'm done with this love thang. Finished!"

Jamie vowed inside that the flow of emotions emanating from his heart would not open to feel love, pain, and this type of loss again. Pleasure was all he would hunt.

$$\Longrightarrow\Longleftarrow$$

Regina wanted Jamie to miss her. She took a leave of absence, and when she returned, no one noticed due to her emphasis on staying out of sight. She watched Jamie's every smooth and agile move while studying his daily patterns from breakfast to lunch to bathroom breaks.

The word was out and floating through the workplace and town that Jamie recently lost his second wife from the grief of losing their baby. Now Jamie was a single man with needs unmet. Both of them needed satisfaction. Even a brief period of loving Jamie was worth the chase. Regina's fire burned inward with desire. Her only thought was to seize and conquer her target. Jamie would be hers if only for a season.

Every day, Jamie would get to the paper mill around 6:55 a.m., and the shift started at 7:05 a.m. He became a pretty popular guy after all the women found out he was twice a widow. The mill became a cesspool for connecting since it was over sixty percent women. He avoided those situations by always playing cool and uninterested.

Female contact was not his goal. The hogs and his kids were all the socializing needed. And from the constant nightmares, anger spells, and clinginess of the younger ones, it was apparent the children were still mourning. Mona and the twins ended up in his bed overnight five times the past week.

Regardless of the warnings from friends and work associates, Raging Regina would not cease her pursuit. She demonstrated a wild, relentless spirit that was indomitable.

"I want you, Jamie. I have given you time. Let me help you forget some of those recurring memories," Regina said as her hands touched him spiritedly with her long, thin fingers from his shoulders to his hips in one long sweep.

"I know your family, Regina."

"Then you know my reputation. I don't usually do this, Jamie—you different, special, and all I need."

Noticing his pause, Regina thrust him into the dark corner of the opened cleaning supply closet and wrapped her leg around his waist with her head buried on his neck. Her hot breath softly upon his ear canal whispered, "You won't regret it, Jamie, not one time."

She succeeded in clenching him in the right spot and at the correct time in his life. That marked the beginning of their special relationship. Within a few escapades, Jamie was hooked. Regina was everything he needed at this point in life. A flame that came with no strings or responsibility attached to it—easy and enjoyable.

Memories of the hospital and last days for both wives were eating him up on the inside. Serena appeared to be visiting him every night after midnight. It seemed as if his heart missed Serena more since Alicia's death.

Jamie consistently visited Serena's grave once a month since her death over ten years ago. He never spoke about his visits to anyone. It was a private affair just for him alone. Many occasions, he would collapse to his knees rubbing the dirt and grass above her, apologizing to Serena about the many women. Other times, he would stretch out next to her plot, jabbering about what was going on with the children and how proud she would be of them. Between Regina and hunting hogs, Jamie distanced himself from the children. The eldest one, Jamison, became the caretaker.

The children began fighting with grades dropping in school until Jamie got a phone call about his youngest girl, Monica, not showing up for school at all. He finally found her sitting cross-legged at the grave of her mother. He joined her, plopping down on his bottom casually.

"Hi," Jamie whispered softly.

"I am not speaking to you. You don't like us anymore, Dad." Monica kept her eyes focused on the horizon beyond the trees. Her head did not move.

He dropped his chin. "That's not true; I love you, Mona. I just don't know how to live anymore. I don't know how to handle all this here pain."

"I didn't do anything to you. Why you have to blame me, Daddy?" She let her glare rest on him. "I wish Momma was alive. Then everything would've been different. You would've been different . . . happy Jamison said. He said he remember you smiled more with Momma when she was alive. He even said you danced with her."

"I wish your momma was here too, Mona. But she's not. I am wrong for how I'm behavin' and skippin' out on you all. I'll do better. Please forgive your old papa; give me another chance to do better."

Monica sat there for a while and stared at the grave with her mother's name on it and the yellow pansies lying across it that she'd brought. She did not say a word but slowly leaned toward her dad's direction, and he put his arm around her shoulder as that sat in the coolness of the evening. The sunrays descended below the big oak trees marking the end of the day.

Jamie made fewer visits to hunt and found a balance. He made fewer rendezvous with Regina and concentrated on his fatherly duties.

One Sunday evening, relaxing at Sean's place to watch the football game, his friends double-teamed him about Regina.

"You real gone, dude, with this woman," Sean his hunting friend proclaimed. "You better watch yourself. The news is travelin' some kinder way."

"Man, she knows the rules," Jamie scoffed. "I'll remind her today . . . we just havin' a good time. I don't need no jive talk goin' round wit' the children hearin'."

"Well, you better get her under control."

Jamie knew he sometimes became so caught up with Regina and their meetings several times a week or more, if he could fit it in, skipping the hog hunts just to be with her at times. It appeared as fireworks every time their bodies connected. He did not like the awakened realization of their meetings getting noticed by others. But if he heard the news from his friends Sean and Shine, then it must be primo gossip on the streets.

"I agree," Shine reiterated. "You losing yourself with this relationship, man. We don't even see you like before and, man . . . and I know your kids miss you. You need to watch it, man . . . she married to a pastor, and everybody know it. It just ain't right, and I just gotta tell you because I'm yer friend."

"Well, I just don't want to rap about this with ya'll, especially right now! We watchin' the game, ain't we?!"

"Damn, alright, it's over . . . I done said what I need to say." Shine sat back on the couch and grabbed another beer.

Jamie pressed back and continued to watch the game as if mesmerized. He did not want to give the impression to the guys that he was worried. They were right—she was consuming his thoughts on and off the job. It was as if he were in handcuffs now and being taken down to the floor. Sometimes, his conscience would leave him uncomfortable when he was away from Regina. Especially now that he began spending more time the children. He knew their affair wasn't right.

He masked the guilt of his relationship with Regina by repeating the rules. If Jamie even got head or tail of news of tension in Regina's home between the Reverend and her, he would leave her alone.

His intention was to play, not to break up their marriage. She had to be mature about their relationship and know that there was no future between them. They were just delightfully enjoying one another's company and fulfilling desires. He wanted to make it crystal clear that he was not mesmerized by Regina's charm and bodacious body. He could put a cease to their relationship at any time effortlessly.

Later that Saturday evening, one mile from the Florida line in a hotel near the beach, Jamie reminded Regina of the initial plan.

"Gina, remember, we are not a couple; we are just enjoying one another very much," Jamie whispered near her ear after he cooled down from their lovemaking sessions.

"I know, Jamie, so stop whining to me about that," Regina blurted, irritated. "Don't ruin the mood. Let's go walk the beach. Please?"

She was helping him forget Serena's and Alicia's recent deaths. It had been almost thirty days since he awoke soaked in sweat in the early morning hours craving Serena's touch. The plan he felt in a single-minded perception was succeeding with keeping their relationship hushed. To the outward world and chatter boxes, Jamie would find out that this warped perception of his was the opposite of what was taking place. Mouths were blabbing in the clubs and homes, heating up the phone lines. They were seen together too often at break time on the job, after work before picking up their children, and most weekends.

Jamie became absent minded to Regina's infrequent remarks about church and consequently skipped over the point that the first lady Regina lying in his arms most evenings was ceasing to attend. Little did Jamie know how seriously the situation had developed.

Jamie's friends were not off the mark. He was under the bewitchment of his huntress. Instead of Jamie controlling and pursuing his prey, he was the hunted one—the wild boar tied down, minus the leathery, brown hair, skin with tusks, and a foaming mouth.

═══ ═══

It was a cool Saturday evening. Jamie and all ten of the children were at the long, maple dinner table, laughing and filling their bellies with barnyard fried chicken, fresh-picked green beans, and mashed potatoes with gravy.

Sitting on the corner seat, Jamison was reaching for another chicken thigh from the bowl while telling one of his side-splitting jokes. He was about to drop the punchline of the joke when everyone stilled due to a demanding fist shaking the frame of the front door. All voices quietened, and no one moved a hair in their chairs as all eyes moved to the front door. Jamie came to his feet quickly to look through the window and observed a group of people he did not recognize at the door. He turned around and shouted to the group of ten confused expressions, "Hey, ya'll, go into the family room and finish eating, alright?"

The kitchen cleared out quickly with the chicken bowl and biscuits traveling into the next room.

Jamison lagged behind and opted to stay, walking in the direction of the rifle.

"No, son, it' all right; you go, too."

"But, Dad?" Jamison wailed. "I'm a big boy."

"Go! Close the door tightly!"

The pounding picked up again.

"I'm coming, so stop beating at my door," he shouted

He snatched the door open and knew it was trouble when he saw Regina.

"Regina, what are you doing here at my house?"

They never visited each whether it was available or not. He would not allow it. He could never make love inside the room of his late wife, Serena, or bring any woman to the house after Alicia died.

"What are all these people doing at my house, Regina?" he snarled to her.

Jamie's backbone stiffened as his eyes glazed over and countenance reddened. Patiently, he shifted from one foot to the other with arms crossed, barring the entrance to his house. His lips pressed tightly together awaiting an answer. It was taking every breath in his body to remain calm.

There were two men and two older women along with Regina gathered on his porch. They looked to be important, but Jamie knew that neither man standing there at his door was Regina's husband. The Reverend's stature and features did not match either of them. Together, the men barged through Jamie's lean frame, pushing their way into the kitchen, and the women pulled Regina in the home who appeared to be stuck in one spot outside on the porch.

Jamie regained his footing and came in, slamming the door and advanced in the direction of the phone and his shotgun. As he was walking, he shouted, "You all have fifteen seconds to clear my home."

One woman, looking to be around seventy with silver hair and no teeth, began to speak crudely and abruptly, "We are here to end this mess between you and the Reverend's wife, Regina. This will end in the name of Jesus."

"Amen!" they all chided in unison.

Jamie abruptly stopped in his tracks and his hunched shoulders slumped as he released a breath loudly. He spun to face them.

The men began to surround Jamie. His stature began to tighten again as he thought about his children in the other room and where his gun was lying. Jamie announced once more, "You need to leave my house. I am asking you nicely

. . ." He never finished his sentence before they started singing loudly, "Lord, send your Holy Ghost Down."

The older women began to pray with distinct fierceness, shoving Regina by Jamie and raising their arms in the air. "God . . . you said what You join together no man can separate; let it not separate and let the Devil be put to shame!"

Repeatedly, they chanted these prayers and many more as they proceeded to go around consistently in a circle. Jamie just gawked in disbelief and shame at Regina and the church folk. The guilt kept him still.

Finally, after some time, the man who was one of the elders at church spoke out loud to Jamie.

"Regina has issued her husband a divorce and hasn't slept in the same room with him or been to the church in almost four months. She barely speaks two words to him, report the Reverend. He even admitted that she curses him in front of the children. This demonic relationship must and will stop for the sake of their marriage and family!"

The man, who was a deacon, elevated his voice to become thunderously loud. He then proceeded to jump up and down, shouting prayers and binding up demons.

Regina, who was in full concentration of squirming and inching her small physique along the wooden wall frames, from the center of attention to leaning against the welcomed backdoor to exit, was jostled into the circle.

Before Jamie could prepare, they forcefully pushed him to join her in the center of the kitchen and coerced them onto their knees. The words they were speaking he could not understand or comprehend. From the sound spewing out their lips, they appeared frightening, and he wanted this to end quickly, so he cooperated.

Out the corner of Jamie's eye, he observed the children creeping out of the family room door to stand huddled with shocked expressions.

He also saw one of them dash in the direction of the shotgun, but he signaled him hurriedly with his hand to stop and that it was okay.

"Go back inside the room and close the door," he shouted over the prayers.

The two teen boys swiftly grabbed the little ones. The eldest was shaking his head with an expression of disbelief as he led everyone back in the room and kicked the door shut. Jamie figured he deserved this and bowed his head.

Chapter 4

Brokenness

After the unwelcomed meeting at his house, Jamie encountered Regina the following Monday. It was two days after the confrontation.

"I'm sorry, Jamie, but they made me come to your house. They threatened to help the Reverend take the kids away from me if I didn't lead them to your house. I have come to quit my job," she admitted as she put items from her locker in a bag.

He fleetingly let his eyes rest upon her face, tightened his lips, and walked away in pursuit of the machine assigned to him. It was five minutes to noon, and the worker was eagerly awaiting a replacement.

She stretched a smile at him as he passed and mouthed in a low volume, "I'll always love you, Jamie," and he hissed air as he continued to walk on as if nothing was spoken.

One of the older women on that dreadful day when the church folk showed imparted some fear into Jamie—one in particular. She asked everyone in the room to leave the house and told Jamie to sit down at the table. Her name was Momma Rubie.

Momma Rubie's distinguished reputation as a wise, discerning, fiery woman was notorious in the neighborhood and nearby towns. A flawless, dark-skinned woman, with the exception of one profoundly deep, angled scar of about eight inches on her right cheek. Rumor had it that she wrestled a wild bobcat in her younger days on the farm and she won. However, before she killed it, the bobcat got one swipe.

She had a full set of teeth at eighty years old and rarely showed it because she never smiled when preaching, and she ministered all the time.

Momma Rubie was 5'2" with bowlegs and a slight bend in her posture. She could out walk the local teen and her thin frame showed it. Her hair was as white as the cotton that lined the fields at harvest, and she kept it neat and curled close to her head at all times.

Momma Rubie sat Jamie down in the nearest seat and pulled up a chair. She starred at him directly in the eyeball and said, "Boy, I know yah hurting n'side and dead like a lifeless deer. De pain of the loss of yah first wife made you this way, and yah just haven't gottin o'er it. Now yah second wife's death has taken whatever life tha's left and 'bout finished yah off 'cause yah feel guilty. I am here to tell yah what de Lord God himself said—'It ain't yer end.'"

Jamie began to slouch down in his chair with his head even lower.

"Son, leave dese women 'lone, especially dis woman, Regina. She's not yours; yah know she's the Rev's wife. She won't fill de hole on de inside that you crave to be filled. Serena's not coming back son—ain't no one can take her place . . . no matter how many ladies yah lay with."

Momma Rubie leaned forward to look Jamie eyeball to eyeball.

"And to let you know that I got dese words directly from God, I'll tell yah what ye wife Serena use to say when yah came home from hog huntin' . . . 'me hog hunter wins again.'"

Jamie sat straight up in the chair; hairs stood up on his arms and legs as his mouth dropped open. He knew Serena or him never shared that with anyone. She just wouldn't, and he didn't. They were always alone when she would jokingly say that to him.

Jamie quickly blurted out, "How did you know that?"

The old lady continued as if he didn't speak a word, "I am tellin' you dis day—right now—God hears and knows yah pain; yer gut cutting aches from Serena and 'licia." She pressed upon his stomach, continuing, "And he weeps wit' you. Let 'em heal yah!"

"He loves you, Jamie!" Momma Rubie wailed on, "and will always . . . even though you've turned yer back on

Him and closed de door since Serena died. Let 'em back in son . . . He'll make you come back alive in yer heart so that you can feel again, son." She touched his heart with her withered arthritic hand. "You just got to give yerself over to Him."

She than began to quote:

"Surely, He has borne our griefs, and carried our sorrows; Yet we esteemed Him stricken, Smitten by God, and afflicted. But, He *was* wounded for our transgressions, *He was* bruised for our iniquities; The chastisement for our peace *was* upon Him, And by His stripes we are healed."

She quoted the words as if she were holding the Bible and reading them verbatim off the pages. Not once did she stumble pronouncing the big words or speak in her usual dialect with the short passage.

"It's in the Bible in Isaiah 53. God loved us so much that He sent His Son to hurt for us so that we can have life. You need to live 'gain on the inside for yer children's sake."

Momma Rubie lifted those short, strong arms with callused hands and threw them around his neck drawing him close. He smelled the scent of turpentine mixed with witch hazel as he fell in her arms, remembering the love and peace of home. It was as if his own momma was wrapping her arms around him. A tear rolled down his cheek as he released his body into her arms. He needed to give his life back to Jesus, especially for his children.

Chapter 5

Survival of the Fittest

J amie avoided all relationships with women for two years. He began to attend church on different occasions, devoting his time to reestablishing a bond with his children and God. Momma Rubie was correct; nobody could take Serena's position, and the single person who was close to reaching that tenderness in his heart and loved his children unconditionally was dead.

Jamie attended the older boys' basketball and football games, participating in parent conferences and, for the little ones gave, important lessons on hog hunting. Anything to stay busy when he was not with his buddies chasing the wild boar with fierceness.

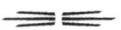

Wild hogs are challenging to hunt because they have such a keen sense of hearing and smell. Their muscular bodies account for their strength and speed, as well as brutality with their sharp tusks that reach outward five inches or more. A few guys on various hunts received permanent injuries chasing hogs, and one even died after an angry, 400-pound hog scurrying for his freedom pounced on him and his weight crushed his breastbone. That hunt reawakened us to the importance of being fast, agile, observant, and aware of the dangers of this sport. Wild boars have above average intelligence and the hog is the fourth most intelligent animal in the world, after humans, apes, and dolphins. Hogs can easily identify danger and to turn the hunter into the hunted.

One hunt down around Homerville, Georgia, near the state line, reminded us of the intelligence of a wild boar.

My friend Shine was answering a call from a family who was struggling with a herd of wild hogs eating their crops and destroying land. I went with him to check it out and help.

"This here is a huge crop of coffee. I see why he's concerned," I said.

"Yeah, and he will pay big dollar if we can help."

Sean, who slept all the way and was now bright eyed, exclaimed, "I'm down wit' dat. Let's go."

We grabbed our gear and prepared our dogs in the cage for business. In no time, our trail dogs picked up the scent.

"Man, there's a lot of them out here. Be careful," Shine whispered. "It's some babies, too. Look over dere."

We glanced toward a thick brush at the remains of a piglet without the head. As we trampled, we were cautious not to rattle leaves and branches as the sky darkened and our overhead light became obliterated with mature trees.

Two hundred yards into the thickened perimeter, we met our catch in a turf war with four other hogs visible through the trees. There were also a couple of piglets running about.

"Alright, boys!" Sean exclaimed and then spat a stream-line of tobacco chew. "I told you we would need these rifles this time. Let's kill some hogs."

"Okay, but we stick together. I'll take out the big tusker, while ya'll aim for the other, and remember don't go near those damn piglets!" Shine blurted in a low voice. "We don't need no mo' trouble than what we got."

The biggest boar, black with short hairs, was no more than 400 pounds. We inched across a small creek, and my foot hit a large branch with a rustle loud enough to spook the two battling boars. We entered, and Sean and Shine were able to get off their shots, which landed the two duelers, while I limped the right-of-way and tipped a third from behind.

We hunched and waited, observing the target boar that was dropped and his opponent; the other two got away along with the piglets. We listened, as the sounds of the escaping boars crashing through the undergrowth grew fainter and farther away. The boars that were shot had not moved an inch, so we cautiously approached on foot.

When we got within a few feet of the larger wild hog, one of the stray boars came out the woods charging our way with preparation for a fight. This boar, despite the gunshot, patiently waited for us to get near his ambush position. With two fiery discharges from the rifle, we scared him off, while one other went down. We figured this group was probably dueling over breeding rights.

Assuming the leader was lifeless when poked and prodded several times with the rifle, we prepared to hog tie 'em. A piglet appeared from the nearby trees as I reached a little too close to the pointed edge of a hog's claws. Impromptu movement as a squealing cry for help left that piglet's mouth awakened my four-legged opponent to swipe, allowing the razor-edged claws to pierce my skin, tearing my forearm.

That pain of the skin tearing and my yelping as I held on to the handcuff clasped to the wild hog's leg to avoid more injury would always be at my forebrain. This caused the need for almost twenty stitches that fall day. But I was determined to conquer my fears and lick my wounds. I would not let one injury stop my lifelong love. I am a hog hunter until the day I close my eyes.

I looked at my love life in that perspective. I was ripped open and experienced piercing pains for many years, but now those stitches, while inside, helped me to heal. They have disappeared, and when the time comes, I am ready to hunt again.

Charlotte's Trail

Jamie met Charlotte two years and two months later on the job. She was fresh meat at the paper mill and new to the area of Russell County. She was different than all the other women in her habits, because during her breaks, a book always hid her face. As he walked passed, Jamie would notice the titles were related to either business startup or how to invest money. She had long, jet-black hair with long legs and stature of six feet.

Charlotte appeared to be mixed with Cherokee Indian and Black American, which she confirmed later because of her pronounced pointy nose with a hump, high cheek bones, and jet-black hair with dark brown eyes. She had very full lips that enticed him to kiss them. He day-dreamed about her full bustier and banging figure, looking just like a Coke bottle without handles and caramel-brown skin. Jamie liked her ways and the attitude with which she carried herself.

Charlotte's work friend approached Jamie about Charlotte six weeks ago and stirred his interest in her. There were several instances Charlotte passed, giving a "hello," and he did not reply, but turned his head as if he were distracted with another task.

"Are you married?" one of her girls boldly asked?

"Why?" he replied, and walked away.

He felt that she wanted him, and she would hunt until she caught him.

Charlotte approached him on a Friday a month later.

"Hi . . . Jamie—right? "

"Yeah . . . and you're Charlotte."

"That is correct."

"Well, I know your two friends because they have been working at the mill for a while, but you . . . this is a first."

He held out his hand to keep it professional, and Charlotte quickly responded with hers.

"So how's it going being the new one on the block?"

"Good, so far," Charlotte responded.

"Well, glad it's workin' out for yah. Let me know if I can be of some help." Jamie turned and started moving away.

"Umm . . . hold on for a sec . . . can I ask you something?"

"Yeah, sure."

Charlotte cleared her throat and shifted her weight from one foot to the other.

"It would be a great favor if you would go to the company dinner with me this weekend."

"Excuse me?"

Jamie could not believe his ears. Raising his eyebrows, he looked her square in the face.

"I want you to accompany me to the dance. I thought I would take a chance on asking you, just to see if you wasn't taking someone else, and since you in management, surely you plan on going?"

He squared his shoulders with an intention of letting her have it—how dare she think she know his schedule—then paused as she flicked her hair back out of her face and made a small gesture with her lips. Now he was feeling uncomfortable as he shifted from one foot to the other.

"You know, I kinda was goin' to skip this one by the company; I really don't go to these things often."

She dropped her eyes and her head followed shortly as her gaze went to his shoes, and he knew he had to surrender to this sweetness.

The company's formal worker appreciation banquet became their first date. They danced as everyone admired their appearance. Jamie and Charlotte complemented each other very well with their high, dark-haired appearances and height.

Back at the table with the candlelight flickering between the two of them, Jamie asked the question he desired since he laid eyes upon her.

"So, Charlotte, how did you end up in Russell County's mill? You just look too refined for such a place."

"My mother got sick, and I came to see about her. Since I was divorced with no children, it was easy for me to pick up and come. She passed away six months ago, and I was glad I came and was able to spend the time with her. I will never regret it."

"I am so sorry."

"Thank you," Charlotte continued. "I just needed quick income and flexible hours, so I started here. Plus, it is not too far from my mom's house."

"I see." Jamie settled further back in his chair.

Charlotte was a smart, educated, and savvy woman whose goal was to open up an adult daycare for the elderly. She said she would work one more year and then she would have all the money she needed to start a successful business.

Jamie had never dealt with an ambitious, educated, refined woman like Charlotte.

"Charlotte, what do you see in me? I don't appear to be your type; I am just a country boy who loves to hunt hogs and is a father to ten children."

They were at one of the popular restaurants in town having a late dinner, tucked away in a dimly lit corner sitting face to face. Charlotte and Jamie had been dating exclusively for almost six months.

"Well, to me, you are like a fine wine. You got some years on you, which have given you wisdom and true-life experience. You're strong and charming—with a hint of sweetness," She said, winking. "You are just different from the average guy. You got your own place and car, and you're obviously smart enough to go get additional schooling—why else would you have the title of assistant foreman!"

"Well, that's true," said Jamie. He grinned wide and chuckled.

He beheld her lavished appearance of thick, black hair pulled into a bun on top of her head, the gold hoops dangling in her ear and perfect, polished lips moving to encourage him, but not go overboard about her feelings. He respected that and felt it was definitely time for his move.

Leaning forward slowly, he lifted his elbows onto the table and said, "I'm getting older, and I been around the block many times; I know what I want in a woman, and you are it."

Jamie moved his chair closer to the table and Charlotte. Signaling the waiter to bring the long-stem wine glasses and bottle of Champagne, he took a breath in as the sound of the liquid filled the glass. Feeling a little jittery, Charlotte lifted the glass for a sip. Jamie reached for Charlotte's hand and squeezed it gently, singing the words so softly, "Charlotte, will you marry me?"

Gasping and sputtering over the sip of wine in her mouth, Charlotte's skin tone changed from reddish brown to almost purple in a matter of seconds.

While shaking in her stacked-heel red shoes, Charlotte's brain cells were swirling and processing during those precious seconds the theory of her age along with the factor of his 10 children, now adults . . . finally, her mind settled on the fact that no issues had arisen. Marriage had no guarantees, and she had been dating the same man for almost 7 months . . . so why not?

"Okay . . . umm . . . yes, yes, I will!"

He grinned, jumped up, and pulled her from the plush seat for a kiss to seal the deal. Then, he reached inside his jacket, produced the small, simple solitaire and slid it upon her finger.

They decided on a small ceremony at the courthouse three weeks later. Charlotte was pregnant within two months. Jamie took care of her and remained calm, smothering all his anxiety and flustering thoughts from the past with Alicia and his beloved Serena.

Jamie worked grueling hours to ensure that Charlotte did not have any needs. She ceased to work four months after the announced pregnancy due to her delicate state. During that free time, Charlotte was able to get her plans together for the adult day care and opened it three months later.

Jamie was now 52 years old and was determined to do it right. Charlotte was 44. All of Jamie's children were adults when he married Charlotte. The twins and baby girl, Monica, graduated from high school and were attending college.

Jamie decided to move into the home Charlotte inherited from her mother, with the agreement that they were going to buy a bigger one together. This time around, Jamie intended on being faithful and attentive. He suffered through many difficult experiences to know that he needed a change in pattern when it came to marriage.

He kept the property and all that Serena and he acquired. The children lived in it, but they knew not to touch their mother's and his room and belongings as their father demanded. Charlotte was not aware, but he went to the house at least twice a month to see the children and look at Serena's belongings. It gave him peace to once in a while look upon and hold her things.

Roger was born healthy and vibrant one fall day in 2003. He filled the house with peace and joy. Roger kept both of them on their toes the first fifteen months with his inquisitiveness and vibrant energy, and it appeared he did nothing but strengthen their bond. Laughter filled the air along with bottles of formula, poop-filled diapers, and restless nights. Everyone adjusted, and life was good.

Charlotte was a loving, praying, and God-fearing woman, which encouraged Jamie to stay faithful. She was always quoting scripture and wanting to set good examples for her friends and other familiar faces. Yes, she was shy, but bold at the same time. There were only one huge draw back . . . girlfriends.

Charlotte believed in having and maintaining close friends. Some of them were friends from when she worked at the mill and others were neighbors who helped her when her mom was alive and presently working with her at the new adult daycare business.

They appeared to be friendly and productive friends, or at least he was deceived into believing from the brief times he met them. The only issue was there was always a friend around or on the phone as if Charlotte couldn't function without some contact with one of them. Jamie decided to confront her about it.

"Charlotte, we need more privacy. I like your girl-friends, but when I come home, I only want to see you. "

"I'm sorry, Jamie. I didn't realize how invasive they were to our relationship. I will respect your wishes. Please forgive me?"

Charlotte fell into his chest, flinging her arms around his neck for a deep hug. Her hands cradled the unshaven face and pressed her lips to his in forgiveness.

"No worries; honestly, I just wanted to point it out. You forgiven—okay? Now what's for dinner? I'm starving."

Before, Charlotte's crew of girlfriends were very attached and like family—sisters to her. Before meeting Jamie, she gained a closely knit circle of girlfriends who assisted her with her mother's needs, getting the job at the mill, and even her hook up to her husband. She would find a balance between her social life and marriage.

The four girlfriends came over Saturday morning. Since Jamie left to hunt hogs at the crack of dawn, Charlotte felt it was safe to invite them over for brunch. Char is what they called her.

"Char, we hate to tell you this, but this is what's been in the air—"

"I swear she ain't lying," another friend broke in.

"What? Just spill it and stop jibber-jabbering!"

"Fine, girlfriend, but what they are saying is that Jamie is sleeping with another female, and they caught her slapping his butt in the break room."

Charlotte dropped the boiler filled with water she was holding back onto the stove.

"Repeat that . . . ?" The room seemed to spin, with her heartbeat intensifying its thud in her chest.

Trina, another miniature friend at 4' fully, wide-eyed and chirpy, chimed in from the corner, "Honestly, that's the rumor that he is running with some young chick with a nose piercing."

"Hey, girls, this is Char here—this can't be true. You got it wrong. I hold my man with better respect than this, and Jamie wouldn't do this. You got it wrong, but thanks for the tip."

"Alright, Char, but I swear, this is what is goin' round, and if it's goin' round, there got to be some truth to it somewhere! You better find some way of checking this thing out, 'cause you don't want to look like a fool . . ." Tina finished with her snapped fingers in the air.

"Wait, hold on," Charlotte piped in. She held her hand out, palm facing outward, toward Tina. "You goin' too far . . . I ain't going to look like no one's fool. I can handle it . . . cool it . . . and let's change the subject, or you can leave . . . all of you." She held her arm out with her index finger pointing out like a gun and panned it in front of all four of them while gesturing her head to the side and curling one side of her lip.

Everyone hushed and looked directly at her. The room fell quiet with no sound except the baby in the homemade crib, gurgling and kicking his legs up. Suddenly, they all burst out laughing and the sassiness was over.

"Girl, what you got to eat?" one of them yelled out.

Charlotte kept the testimony of gossip in the back of her mind. She did not confront Jamie directly that day because there was no proof.

"What's with the fifty questions, Charlotte?"

"I'm just asking where ya'll went hog hunting at, Jamie. It is just an innocent question."

"You ask me every time I go now, where before you didn't! What's wrong with you?"

Blowing a breath, she blurted out, "I was told you cheating on me, Jamie."

"Oh, so one of your hussy, little friends told you this lie, and you going to believe it?"

"My friends don't lie!"

"Really? Well, since you believe them, then what are we doing?"

"Exactly, you need to leave if you can't be honest. I will not be disrespected!"

"No problem." Jamie walked to the back and threw some clothing in a bag. The front door shook the frame of the house from the force as he swung it shut.

$$\Longrightarrow\Longleftarrow$$

The ladies have never been a problem for a hunter like me to attract. There was a sassy sexy female named Janette who was pressing in on me, but I spoke to her earlier in her schemes, frankly relaying that I was married and not interested. Well, now it is time to remove that image. I showed her kindness when turning her flirtatious behavior away. Now I could have used all the flirtation and more because I needed something new to make this hurt simmer down.

Janette was great with her drop-dead figure, front and back, and smooth cocoa skin with bright white teeth and oval face. She had a little of Asian American in her, which explained the slightly slanted eyes and jet-black, short-cropped hair, but she was no Charlotte. I was determined to do it right . . . until that day . . . that moment when Charlotte believed her friends over me.

$$\Longrightarrow\!\Longleftarrow$$

When Jamie walked out slamming the door, he could hear Charlotte in the background yelling, "You'll be back!"

Jamie was not one to fuss. Never was. He dialed Sean's number. He only packed a small duffle bag with his essentials and work clothes.

"Sean, hey, I need a place to lay over for a while. Thanks."

Charlotte put Jamie out of the home that night, and he stayed away for five years.

Chapter 6

The Hunt Continues

"Thanks, man, for letting me come over and stay. I don't know what got into that woman, but she told me to leave, and that's what I did."

"Sorry, man . . ." Sean said. "Want a beer?"

"Yeah, yeah, pass me a couple of them."

"Women and their friends. I can't believe I'm goin' through dis shit again. I'm done wit' this relational stuff," Jamie hissed as he took an extra-long gulp then reclined back and kicked up his heels on his friend's sofa.

"Take it easy, man—you know you don't drink."

"I'll be alright," Jamie snarled.

Jamie began seeing Janette two weeks later. Charlotte continued to make accusations and Jamie ignored by avoiding her unplanned visits with a change in his schedule.

Jannette was easy to deal with. She was not a demanding chick. At minimal, to get her engine running required a bottle of gin and the latest band or good disc jockey to get her feet skipping. Jannette loved to party.

Jannette was a young country girl, and she liked to drink and move her body. Jamie pulled up in his big, black F-150 with shiny rims and blew the horn. Jannette and he were dancing tonight.

"You look so sexy. I could eat you up. Let's go have some fun."

They danced and drank all night until the sun rose. Then Jamie spent the night until mid-Sunday morning at her place.

Jamie made the turn for Sean's place. His head felt like a tough piece of pork shoulder receiving tenderization. As he passed Mt. Gilead church, he saw Charlotte with his son, who was now five years old, getting out of the car. She did not see him as he cruised by because her back was turned as she entered the church. His heart sunk, and he exhaled loudly enough to cause the hairs on his hands to dance as his knuckles clenched the wood-grain steering wheel.

When they started this fight, he was unaware it would last this long. Two weeks max was what he thought. Now the feud added up to over three years that he has been out of his son's life and separated from Charlotte. The boy barely knew him. Charlotte just refused to bend to good reason and admit that her girlfriends were wrong.

Stubborn was not the word for Charlotte. That expression was too tame. More like stupid, pig headed, and prideful.

Charlotte came to his job and declared publicly that he would be back in her home again in front of his staff. "You will need me before I need you, and you'll be begging to come back," she spewed at him in first soprano with her finger pointing in his face. That incident changed the tone of their relationship. Jamie's manliness would not allow him to go back.

He soon would be getting his new place a few miles up the road. He'd saved up enough money for the down payment. He also vowed to start picking up his son and developing a relationship. Monica, his youngest daughter, said she would help him do that by picking Charles up and bringing him to see Jamie. Jamie did not want to deal with Charlotte.

Jamie turned in the driveway of his friend doublewide trailer. He put the car in park and was about to open the door when his vision blurred and he felt severe pain in his right jaw. His head bobbed to the rear and then fell forward onto the horn as he collapsed.

Chapter 7

Surrendering

J amie woke up at Columbus Medical Center in ICU with aching body pain, a small bandage around his head, IVs, and monitors beeping in his ear, reminding him that he was breathing. The doctor told him shortly afterward that what he experienced was a myocardial infarction . . . a stroke.

"Just rest, Mr. Patterson, and let your body heal."

As the hours and days passed, Jamie began to confuse his nights and from days, which affected his sleeping and waking pattern. He started to notice there was only one side moving on his body when shifting his weight in the bed toward the right.

On the left side, there appeared to be no sign of sensation, feeling was absent, along with no movement of his legs and arms. Nothing! Those body parts were just lying there like a limp piece of meat, numb, and with all his effort applied to lift them, he could not so much as bring his hand to his mouth. He just did not feel any sensation.

"Heeellpp! Please help me. I can't feel anything. Oh, God, what is wrong with me?!" he exclaimed at the top of his lungs.

In seconds, his room was full of people in white scrubs and jackets. Charlotte was sitting in the chair next to his bed nodding and leapt to her feet to calm him, but she was quickly overtaken by several frantic uniformed persons who booted her from the room. They immediately injected a needle, and within five minutes, Jamie's heartrate quietened, and somehow, he felt as if he floated through the air. Minutes later, his eyelids felt like lead and closed shut to his sweet whistles to rest.

When he awoke, he glanced to his right and there she sat with her body leaned over to one side, her head rested on a small square pillow. Even in disarray, Charlotte was beautiful. Her eyes were shut in deep slumber.

"Charlotte," Jamie called in a soft, feeble voice, but to him, it appeared to be earth-shaking loud. He spoke her name four times before she heard him. She slowly lifted her eyelids to reveal her light-brown pupils, and she leapt up on her feet, her eyes filled bubbled over with glee.

"Jamie!" She leaned down and planted a kiss on his crinkled forehead. She sauntered to the door, a quick glance back in assurance, teeth showing from ear to ear as she turned once more, then next dashed out the room, vehemently singing, "Nurse, nurse, he is awake. Please come check . . . he is responding to me!"

The nurse came in and checked his vitals.

"We are happy you are feeling better, Mr. Patterson. Your vitals are good and strong. I will get the doctor."

"Thank you, nurse," Jamie replied. "May I have some water please; I'm so thirsty."

Thirty minutes later, the doctor came in and checked his reflexes and how quickly his verbal responses were to questions given. He noticed and admitted that nothing moved on Jamie's left side.

"We are going to run some more tests, and then the plan is rehabilitation to help you adjust and improve your coordination and strength, Mr. Patterson, but honestly, the movement might take some time to return."

"No, doc—you mean I might be like this for years?!" Jamie exclaimed.

"It depends on the extent of the damage to the brain and how it affects your nervous system," the doctor told him standing at his side.

"Doctor, I am determined to do whatever it takes to get my movement back so I can hunt hogs again."

"I am glad to hear you admit that and agree to my ordering you to rehabilitation therapy to work on your daily living skills, strength, walking, and speech. We will get you moved as soon as I perform all the tests and get the results."

"Alright, doc, thank you."

Charlotte never spoke of their history; she just looked at him that day after the doctor left and confessed, "Jamie, I am sorry. I will take care of you, so don't worry 'bout anything. I know you may be thirsty and a little hungry. Let me go ask or see if you can get something to eat or drink?"

His pampering days began. He basked in all the attention from Charlotte and the nursing staff until the first day of rehabilitation.

Rehabilitation

The hog knows when to give in when it is caught. The fight goes out of it when the twitches, squirms, squeals of distress reside after being handcuffed. Finally, it gives this gut-wrenching screeching sound as it brings its head to one side. It's as if it can smell death before it happens.

In rehabilitation, I felt like one of those wild boars I'd caught in the past. I was pinned down, handcuffed, and any tactic I utilized could not free me from the confinement of this condition I found myself in. Helpless, hopeless, and prepared for death is the feeling that was surfacing.

The first day at the rehabilitation center was beyond difficult. The people did not respond to every call when the buzzer was pushed, which became overly frustrating after 48 hours. Charlotte was allowed to come for a couple of hours that first afternoon after the hospital release and transfer. She helped to get everything settled in and took care of simple paperwork demands before she was encouraged to leave. The staff wanted all new clients to get accustomed to the schedule of therapy in the morning and afternoon.

After two hours of holding my bowel and bladder too long, my desire was to call her to check me out this hell hole. I detested waiting until someone finally came after pulling a damn cord and sitting in the wheelchair watching the door. It was beyond frustrating to be unable to satisfy an urge because you can't get up from a wheelchair.

After twenty-four hours of being so distraught and urgently curbing the desire, I yanked open the bathroom door and rolled inside. With my strong single hand and foot, I attempted to pull myself up. For the first seconds, in half stance, it went well, but within seconds, my weak knee collapsed with my hand slipping from the grab bar, and before I could curse, well, my six-foot frame was sprawled on the marble floor.

≡≡

"Dammit, help me," he screamed.

He lay like a block of timber, unable to roll. He forgot to lock his wheelchair, and it moved farther in the opposite direction. The chair was of no use for stability to help him pull his body up. He probably lacked the strength anyway with one hand. Distraught tears of helplessness escaped from the corners of his eyes. What seemed like thirty minutes was in reality less than five minutes before staff arrived with a Hoyer lift to lift him off the floor.

"It took two people and a machine to get you off the floor. Please, Mr. Patterson, do not get up until someone comes. We don't want something worse to happen to you like a broken hip or a head injury. Please, sir, wait for assistance."

"I tried, but when I got to pee, I got to go."

"You have a urinal there by the bed, sir. Please use it if no one comes fast enough. And for accidents, this is why you utilize these special diapers."

Jamie gave the nurse a glare and, seething, blurted, "Get out! You must think I am a fool if you think I'm goin' to piss in my pants. I'm still a man. A man in my right mind, you know!"

"Sir, no one has implied that—"

"Get out!" Jamie interrupted, raising his voice louder.

More staff rushed up the hall when the nurse hurriedly shut the door of Jamie's room.

Jamie held the weight of his moist face with both hands as the door was pulled shut. He forgot how to fight for life. He was moved to the rehabilitation unit, and instead of battling for strength and movement, he surrendered to his inner demons encouraging defeat.

He was a hog hunter unable to hunt—half a man with a useless arm and leg—of no use to anybody. He was feeble, an invalid who couldn't even pee by himself. He slumped back further in bed where they put him and groaned inward while weeping aloud, desiring Serena.

———

The doctors started giving Jamie an antidepressant, and after a couple of days, his spirits seemed to lift. He started attending the recreational activities they had during breaks in therapy and even learned how to move his wheelchair independently by using his right side which was his strong leg and arm.

Two days after his fall, Jamie got a pleasant surprised which broadened his outlook on his condition and spear-headed his determination to live again. It was a surprise visit from Monica. She knocked on the door and entered the room one early morning right after breakfast. It was his fourth day in rehab.

"Daddy," she said, giving him a huge hug as he sat in the wheel chair. "I rushed over as soon as I heard!" Monica declared. "Why did you tell them not to tell me? You are more important than class, Daddy!"

Jamie wanted her to complete her training with her work and told everyone not to tell her.

"I'm fine. I'm still living, ain't I?" Jamie held up his right arm in sarcasm, with his artery jumping rapidly under the base of his jaw at the sight of Monica sauntering through the door. It was as if Serena were with him again. She looked just like her mom.

"Aw, Daddy, stop your pretending." She rushed over to pull him close. A flood of tears sprung from his eyes, uncontrollably soaking the back of Monica's shirt. She was his Mona—his baby girl, the last gift her mom gave to him before she died.

"I love you and want the best for you. Don't worry about me. I'm going to be okay," he muttered, leaning back in the bed pillow.

"I know you are, you hog hunter. I'm just going to hang around a little to give you a shove in the butt."

"Wait . . . you are not goin' to do dat . . . hanging around this place full of invalids when you need to be studying and stuff."

"I'm not taking no for an answer. It is not an option. You stuck with me comin' almost every day or so."

Monica came every day along with Charlotte regularly in the afternoon. Jamie started to fight again to regain his independence. He had been there twenty-one days. He learned how to dress independently, including shoes and socks, how to get in and out of bed, manage to get from the wheelchair to the toilet and in and out the shower in a tight space. Jamie became strong enough to be independent with all his self-care and functional transfers during the day and night and did not need to use the call button as long as he had his wheelchair.

When it was time for his release, he did not create conflict when Charlotte insisted he come to the house they lived in together many years ago before their big fight.

Occupational and physical therapy resumed there at Charlotte's, now his home, to assist with daily skills for dressing, bathing, transfers, and use of safety equipment. Soon the wheelchair was rarely used, as Jamie walked with a quad cane in his daily surroundings. Occupational therapy assisted Jamie to utilize and regain some movement in his left hand, arm, and shoulder. He also learned how to write his signature and eat with a utensil with his right hand. Initially, it was a battle, for he was biologically a lefty.

Life was improving and joy was returning to his heart. He was indeed thankful for every day he could move by personal strength and be independent.

"Happy birthday, Dad!" Monica smiled and gave him a kiss on the cheek. It was September 29. He was 69 years old.

"I feel 69; look at all this gray that came overnight on my big head!"

"Oh, we know you earned every speckle," Monica replied in giggles. "This is why I brought you a gray-looking cake."

"What! You better get out of here wit' dat!" He fired back.

She began slowly raising the lid, spewing, "Get ready, you old Hog Hunter," and removed it completely with a toothy grin to reveal his favorite German chocolate cake with a single candle on top. Mona chuckled and lit the singing candle.

"Okay, make a wish."

It had now been a year later since he was released from the rehab center, and he still did not have full use of his left arm. Mona passed the knife to him, and he reached out with his right hand and made a generous cut down the center.

"You know I am terrible at this."

"Well, I think it is the perfect cut. I'll take that slice if you think you can't handle it!"

"The birthday boy is supposed to get the first slice, so don't go getting yo' hopes up."

She slid his plate to the corner of the mahogany table where he was sitting.

"Daddy," she said, passing him a fork, "are you happy . . . being here in this house—you know?"

Jamie's grin disappeared as he pushed his cake away and dropped his chin. He rubbed his forehead as he prepared to speak.

"Mona, it took me a long time to let go of the past pain and have a little faith. Let God handle thangs. It is very difficult when the pain is so deep. Every day, I let a little pain go—until one day, I woke up and it was completely gone."

Jamie pressed his back into the chair with a sober look and continued, "I am thankful for Charlotte. Charlotte has put up with a lot from a broken, disabled man. She didn't even mind when your mama's sister, brother, and cousins came over to the house from out of town to visit me a couple of days ago. She is a strong woman. God is definitely in control."

"I see, Dad."

"No, let me finish . . . 'cause you know I have not made the best choices in my life. I know you remember that after the death of your mother I became hollow, like a depressed piece of sunken wood with no life and no desire for it. Then, when 'licia died I cracked, like an egg into a bowl on contact."

Jamie dropped in his chin. "That guilt was just too much for me to handle. I felt I was the cause of her death. So I would go to the club drinking if I wasn't hunting . . . and you know I didn't touch the stuff when your mother was alive. I became so popular at the juke joints until the fellas and gals bought my dranks and my songs. I'd proclaim and sway:

If you don't love, you don't lose no one.

When you don't lose no one, you don't cry—

And you can't damn well cry, if you hunt hogs—

Only drink beer and laugh!"

He continued, "I am sorry, baby girl, because I should have been there more for you all kids. Ya'll lost her, too. Please forgive me?"

"I do, Pops." Monica came over to hug him. "It's okay."

Monica pushed the German chocolate cake to him after she kissed him on the cheek.

"Well, now I laugh more without the drinkin' and partying. I still think about your mom some nights and drive over to visit her grave every once and awhile, but I allow room in my heart for Charlotte. God gave me peace in that area after a long time of carryin' that pain. I have got healing and comfort in that area and it took me over 40 years to get it. God gave me a second chance."

"Dad, you really have grown. You' old geezer, it's about time!"

"Aw, shush yo' mouth, Mona, and pass me the fork, so I can give this cake what it deserves . . . a good eatin'."

Bellows of laughter rung out as she slid him a fork and napkin.

"Now don't you go following in my footsteps with this dranking and partying. Your brothers and sisters are all doing well like you. I want you to continue to do the same, Mona."

"Well, Dad . . . you know your blood runs thick in my veins . . ."

"I know . . ." he whispered.

"For I am truly . . . my hog hunter father's child."

Chapter 8

Conclusion

My hair is like salt and pepper with curls now. My eyes are weary, and bifocals are needed for me to see anything. They say surgery is needed for cataracts in one of them. I am 69 years old now, I continue to walk with a cane, and I do not have full use of my left arm.

It took me a long time to let go of the past, the pain, and have faith. Let God handle it, is what they would often proclaim. It took nearly my whole lifespan, but now I understand. I give thanks for my third wife. Month after month, as I returned to the home we originally shared with so much peace and joy when we welcomed our newborn son, I began to envision her in a different light, to appreciate her commitment and daily determination to improve the life of someone who abandoned our marriage and family.

My son Charles was able to build a loving father–son relationship after few months of being home, because of Charlotte's continued kindness, even when I was absent. She did not poison his mind. Present day, he sings the dad off his lips and will patiently listen to my advice with respect. I bless her for this gift.

Charlotte also didn't mind when Serena's brother and cousins came back to the house like I asked to offer their assistance in fixing some things that my disabled body and hands could not do anymore. She allowed them to take over the house and assist however they wanted with cooking, cleaning, and trimming hedges, cleaning floor boards, and mowing the lawn. I realized then how much of the help I was not able to give daily due to all these disabilities, and I wept because she does still love me. God is definitely in control.

In the past, my lips would easily form my famed motto after a couple of beers with my hog hunting buddies:

If you don't love, you don't lose no one.

If you don't lose no one, you don't cry.

When you don't cry, you hunt ferocious hogs,

Drink good beer and laugh hard.

Well, I have let some chuckles free pretty often. I also still cry and hug my pillow every once in a while thinking of my Serena. But I allowed room in my heart for Charlotte. I thank God that I got not only a second chance, but with my history, more likely a fortieth chance at love, forgiveness, and grace.

My eleven children are aware of some of the past bumps and bruises I have endured, because I believe in the importance and power of history. Sharing my account will help them avoid creating their own foolish history and allow my offspring to go beyond those ignorant mistakes.

"Remember, avoid those pitfalls, and pass it along," I vehemently instruct them. My desire to share this pain and shame with anyone wise enough to hear my testimony and apply the learning to their life is deeply rooted.

I, Jamie, was the hog hunter who had a hole in his heart and didn't think no one could fill it back up. I was the man filled with aches and emptiness; the hunter shackled—handcuffed—and dead inside since that dreadful day I received the horrific news on my knees in that ammonia-scented hospital that my Serena took her last breath.

It took almost a life time to rekindle this serenity and significance about life now, almost 40 years. I live, I love, and I truly laugh. Momma Rubie was right. May she rest in peace. God forgives, so you can let go. Leave it all at the altar.

mirrorbuzz99@gmail.com

www.ingramcontent.com/pod-product-compliance
Lightning Source LLC
Chambersburg PA
CBHW060645130626
46555CB00002B/965